Abridged But Out There

Six months of Simon

a novel

ܐܒܪܝܕܓܕ

Grey Gorman

ܓܪܝܓܘܪܡܢ

EverydaySanctuary
Denver

Abridged but Out There: Six Months of Simon
© 2004 Grey Gorman

All rights reserved. No part of this book may be reproduced or transmitted in any form for profit without prior written permission from the publisher.

Printed in the United States of America by EverydaySanctuary Publications.

EverydaySanctuary email addresses and ES messenger screenames are copyrights of EverydaySanctuary Publications and are used with permission.

Avestan fonts © 2000 Department of Classical and Near Eastern Studies at the University of Minnesota used with permission.

Excerpts from *the Karamazov Brothers* by Fyodor Dostoevsky, edited and translated by Ignat Avsey @ 1998 Oxford University Press reprinted with permission.

www.everydaysanctuary.net

ISBN 0-9761900-0-1

Any copies or editions of this book sold or printed for sale by publishers other than *Everydaysanctuary Publications* are sold in violation of copyright and the wishes of the author and the publisher.

Printed on recycled paper

For Conni

Note from the Publisher

EverydaySanctuary Publications has been established as a zone for internet-accessible works by writers, visual artists and musicians with samples and/or complete versions of works available for viewing or download.
All creators retain full copyright control.

With this novel EverydaysSanctuary has made available the materials in a manner agreed consistent with the spirit of the principle character.

This has been established as: the split-profit sales of printed publication and the freely internet-available digital publication through the everydaysanctuary website. All money received from sales of this work will be split as: 50% of profits above cost donated in the name of Simon to approved charities; remaining 50% split evenly between publisher and the author. Profits after cost have been defined to include all money gained above the costs of printing, shipping, website operation and management, and publicity in relation to the novel. Any printed editions sold to charitable social service or educational insititutions done so at cost. Any donation of editions to charities may be done by publisher or author after profit-split.

Equal percentages of profit donated in the name of Simon Spellman will be distributed to organizations designated and linkable on www.everydaysanctuary.net.

Any similarity between these published names, email addresses and messenger screennames to real or accurate names, addresses and messenger programs of other domains and internet service providers is purely coincidental.

There are no contactable, real people on the recieving end of these EverydaySanctuary addresses and ES messenger screenames.

The addresses and names within this publication have been altered enough from those of real persons as to prevent any undue harassment or infringement of privacy, particularly to any minors involved.

Additionally, following the form of the original printing, we have avoided any attempts at listing or explaining any referenced materials herein or the allusion of works within the public sphere, simply as it would detract from the story and its ability to impact and undoubtably would not be done fully and fairly.

Lastly, all proper places and locations that decidedly will not give away the identities of any persons have remained. When in doubt, and only when necessary, specifics have been replaced with ambiguities.

The fact that this story is set within the recent everyday of millions of souls is truly what allows it to impact so deeply and personally. It is with our hopes that it will be able to continue to impact countless more in the future, around Boston, and around the world.

EverydaySanctuary Publications

Introduction

Simon

Seen like this, he was still just a bunch of data. Not yet a full program.

Maybe that's all any of us are.

But I feel like Simon wanted to be, as he would have probably said, a wicked awesome program.

I know that now.

In the end all he would be was an assorted collection of miscellaneous data. But he was already a better collection than so many, with years on him.

I do this, introducing Simon to you all, to relieve myself of a lot of the grief I suppose. But I do think that there is some good that could come from it.

So pardon my harshness and brashness for a moment, but this directed to anyone who will criticize this action and will tangent off of this sweet person lost and would rather sum him up in a one-sided pretty-picture, online profile-lack-of-depth, obituary-like sound-byte, to be held and then easily discarded: To hell with you. To hell with you right here and now, and stop trying to take the rest of us there with you.

I know he's a ticket stub for you. That comparison works on so many levels and it makes you uncomfortable and almost sick, doesn't it? Thrown away easily by some of you. Kept for a while by others. Held dear by a few, but eventually put into a box of other semi-sentimental things.

You don't want to admit it. And you'll attack me for being so rude. But you'll do that because you know down to your neglected core that I'm *dead* right.

National Geographics have a longer shelf life than Simon will have for many of you.

Instead of learning lessons from this person, you will mourn your mortality that Simon did not have a choice in reminding you of. You will try to mold him into something that he was not, or wasn't only, and in order to silence your worry and fear that you know you're the principle cause of.

I know. Because I've been there. I've been the worst example, which is why I'm doing this now. Simon has so quickly confronted me with so much of myself neglected and forgotten. Simon had that problem too. But he was getting over it. He was working himself better. And now so am I.

Thank you Simon.

To the majority whom that that does not apply, please read on.

Simon came into my office for help. I told him I was busy, told him to make an appointment. I only looked up for a second. But I caught his eyes. How I wish I hadn't caught his eyes.

He said he'd wait until I was finished if he could. I said whatever and tossed him a National Geographic. He went into the other room. I figure he got bored with it after all the pictures, because he left it open to a story upside down.

He left his bag and he left his computer, too. But he took his skateboard.

The driver left nearly a dozen empty bottles on the bar, but took his keys. And he forgot to care about anyone else in those important few moments.

Simon left his board and took to the air, but his body forgot to keep breathing. I hope Simon left his body still thinking he was skateboarding.

A childish part of me inside likes to think Simon's now skateboarding in the sky. That part of me still thinks I can choose what the next card in the deck is if I think hard enough, too.

I need to do this because Simon is not skateboarding in the sky. He is grinding and piping in my head. He deserves to board in any heads he likes. In this one way, at least, I've been deputized as his personal assistant.

I hid his computer and didn't tell them.
I don't know why.
Later his family asked around where it was. I told them that he never took it out. I told them it must have been stolen by someone through all the commotion.

I lied. And I suppose I told the truth, as it were.
I suppose initially, I kept it to keep Simon's privacy.
I kept it later to invade Simon's privacy; because he didn't have any anymore.
And because, somehow I knew, no one else would.

I don't ask for forgiveness but for understanding from anyone discomforted by parts of themselves now out there for the world to see. Simon alluded to so much of himself he felt he lost in a ruined hard drive. I couldn't stand by and have these remaining couple months of him be lost forever in the same fashion.

I do what I can so that he will not be mutated or altered to go along with the fresh scent we would all like to put over this sadness in us.
I won't allow it to come to that, so I do what I can to have Simon speak for himself.

In what may be my last act as a teacher, I do what I can to bring this person back into the lives of many, and I hope many that did not yet know him but who find that they needed a little piece of him.

With respect and hope,

P. Alvérez

Boston, Massachusetts
September 2004

Contents

Note from the Publisher

Introduction

Files from Simon's "My Shiznit" Folder

May

4/29	IM - HotTamale86
5/10	WTF - take four
5/11	anti blog - and so it begins
5/17	email - Tracey Re: WTF
5/17	email - Tracey Re: no subject
5/17	IM - DevilLAX35
5/20	IM - HotBobBaBy02
5/22	email - Ashad
5/24	email - NateDogg36

June

6/3	email - Angie
6/6	email - Jenn
6/7	email - Tracey
6/13	IM - DevilLAX35
6/13	email - Travis Re: wicked nasty
6/13	email - Travis Re: Danielle
6/17	IM - ashad04
6/19	IM - Jennzen
6/22	email - Becky
6/23	anti blog ➢ Antiblog - Trebuchet
6/26	IM - HotTamale86
6/28	IM - Trace08
6/30	IM - Trace08

July

7/1	email - Danielle	
7/2	Antiblog - Piss n Moan	
7/5	Antiblog - Makeshift ab maybe	
7/6	IM - Trace08	
7/9	email - Jenn	
7/12	Antiblog - BC + God of Lit	
7/13	Antiblog - Paine in My Ass	
7/17	Antiblog - Galileoed Common Sense	
7/21	IM - HotTamale86	
7/23	email - Tracey	

August

8/12	Antiblog - Best boobs are breasts	
8/18	Antiblog - Goodbye Tim	
8/23	IM - Trace08	
8/28	email - Tracey	
8/30	Antiblog - Passion and Dispassion	
8/31	email to self - Sorry Becky Backup	

September

9/2	email - Lissa Ann	
9/5	email - Jenn	
9/6	Antiblog - Oy vey	
9/7	Antiblog - Damn Deep	
9/7	Antiblog - Asshole hole hole	
9/8	Antiblog - Back in the Day	
9/9	IM - EQPhreak	
9/11	Antiblog - Makeshift Sanity	
9/12	Antiblog - Deep Ol Fucker	
9/12	Personal Statement rough draft	
9/12	Antiblog - One N Hockey Jen	
9/13	Antiblog - Forever Smitten	

P.S.

9/21

"Words differently arranged have a different meaning,
and meanings differently arranged have a different effect."

Blaise Pascal

Simon's "Shiznit"

Subj:	**Diana IM 4-29**
Date:	Thr. 4/29/2004 9:54:48 PM EST
From:	ssspellman@everydaysanctuary.net
To:	ssspellman@everydaysanctuary.net

castaspell: yo chica
HotTamale86: hey Simon
castaspell: so whats up? finally able to chat with ya :)
HotTamale86: nada...yea
HotTamale86: hablando con mi padre, un momento ¿y tu?
castaspell: hey, how do you do that funkey shit on your puter?
HotTamale86: ok back
HotTamale86: ancient mex secret ;)
castaspell: yea yea be that way :)
HotTamale86: yea I'm just cool that way nah I don't know, just the way my dad set up the computer
castaspell: So yea what was up with that crazy fucker today??
HotTamale86: Yeaa!! no doubt...what the fuck? How can you go from wicked cool to total psycho in two seconds?
castaspell: exactly... its like the drag racing of crazy
HotTamale86: LOL
HotTamale86: why is that like the second the temp gets above 65 the gates open up at the asilums or whatever
castaspell: makes you long for the days of the cool crazy. like smellypaulie remember him?
castaspell: the non agro in for the long haul kind of crazy?
HotTamale86: LOL yea I do
HotTamale86: yea paulie was like the Indy 500 of crazy isnt he
castaspell: damn...you know the lingo, you going redneck on us? Don't let the boyfriend corrupt you too much.
HotTamale86: shut up simon
HotTamale86: :-P
HotTamale86: you know what would be sweet thou?
castaspell: what?

HotTamale86: all handing out handsfree earpeace things to people like paulie, cause then they could look normal when they wanted to, like their just talkin on the phone
HotTamale86: u kno...takin care of busines
castaspell: LOL!!!!
castaspell: no shit!!
castaspell: right on
castaspell: did you see that dude's eyes though? he totally sketched me out
HotTamale86: yea!! that was freaky...like all of a sudden he was looking through you, like u were a 3d puzzle or something
castaspell: Exactly!!! Then boom!
castaspell: least he went off on himself though.
HotTamale86: yea def
HotTamale86: lucky for us
castaspell: Wonder if you can add more options to him, like more RAM or something, he seems to be low in that. :)
castaspell: Like find a hypnotist or something and add more to the floor model
HotTamale86: Yeah! Like you could buy new features or something
castaspell: Yea like cable options, sports package or the all premium movie packages
HotTamale86: look at you, knowing all the fucking terms
HotTamale86: geek
castaspell: whatever. 'hold on, I have to go get myself a soooooyyeee milk from the fridge'
HotTamale86: yea yea
castaspell: promise you wont tell no one but I actually scored pretty high this online geek test
HotTamale86: yea not surprised
castaspell: hey, but yea how bout we mod that guy out so that when you ring a doorbell or something he thinks he's an eight year old girl or something?
HotTamale86: hahaha!!
castaspell: that guy's like the definition of the WTF-factor.
HotTamale86: the what?

castaspell: the What The Fuck Factor. He's like the brandname advertizement for somekind of psycho.
HotTamale86: oh yea
castaspell: so now there's two extremes, cool smellypaulie and the i carry around a fucking coffee stamper in my backpocket so I canbeat myself senseless stupid fucker
HotTamale86: we should give him a hammer next time and tell him to takeit back to the hardware stroe! then maybe he can be done with it!!
HotTamale86: *store
castaspell: LOL!!
HotTamale86: so where you think the keymaster come in?
castaspell: ?who
HotTamale86: the keymaster, some guy I guesss who walks around town with like a 1000 keys on him, my bf told me about him. They all call him the keymaster like in ghostbusters.
castaspell: dunno…would have to see it, can just imagine though.
castaspell: hey what was that book that other dude mentioned after thatguy started going apeshit on himself?
HotTamale86: ah shit….
castaspell: its like running or soemthing…
HotTamale86: Running with Sisscors!!
castaspell: Yes!
castaspell: right on. Gotta check that out. See what they were talking about with the crazies.
HotTamale86: Let me know if you find it, what its all about.
castaspell: def
castaspell: hey, wanna go see a movie this weekend?
castaspell: I'm going with Tim and Trav and the gang .
HotTamale86: can't. working. thanks thou
castaspell: oh well
castaspell: hey gotta jet.
castaspell: Adios bonita chica
HotTamale86: hasta gringo
HotTamale86: :)
castaspell: I know what that one emans!!1
HotTamale86: :D

Subj:	**WTF take four**
Date:	Mon. 5/10/2004 2:08:02 AM EST
From:	ssspellman@everydaysanctuary.net
To:	ssspellman@everydaysanctuary.net

shocking…its time for another WTF…

but seriously, what the fuck? I mean really WHAT THE FUCK? Is there some law dat says that two people both cant like each other, otherwise we all fuckign blow up? Cause yet again superhotcool girl says she valudes my 'friendship' too much to risk losing it. 'I like you like a brother' funny y is that what they say right before never talking to you agian. Ooooooh, so that kind of friend? riiiight.
Y doesnt anyone want me? Angie sure did before we started flirtni and talking…and then boom. Never changes I cant say this to any of the guys, its all about hooking up and shit…but it never goes beyond names dates and places. Why cant I have someone I can talk to like Jenn, but who wants my shit like that Jersey chick or, i dunno? is that too much to ask? what really pisses me off is watching all the guys i know fuck it up with the cool girls…y?? how? what the hell was wrong with them, they want to hang out with your friends, can talk about things past the stupid shit, arnt crying and wining in your ear every othr hour, and actually have some sort of hope gting out of this fucking town and besides the fact theyr hot and want to get on you Mad props to them! Yeaaa, but no were looking for bitches I'm sorry. just wrong isnt it? Fucking fools. I know when I get a girl like that, I'm not going to fuck it up goddamnit

Fucking fools.

<file listed as created and saved May 11, 2004 at 10:38 pm>
                -- GG

New computer time!!!!!!!!!!! ROCK THE FUCK ON!!
"We think this is appropriate for all the hard work you've demonstrated......blablalbalbalbbalablablab" Whatever...,Sweet!!!

I scammed a computer,. So...by stress fracturing an ankle and unable to play and sitting my lazy ass down with some books to keep unbored I scammed a puter!?? What else ya offering???
    ooo and spell correct rock the fuck on!

    A badass MOFO OF A TOY

    But I'll be all cool with it and won't go the fucking lame route like so many other fools. No fucking online journaly bullshit here. I'm so anti blogging. Fucking people can't do anything without other people around. How fucking pathetic. But wait...you can do private entries . So why the fuck do you need it online and have an account and get fucking spam mail from penis people in order to write to yourself privately? assholes
    What the fuck is the point of a journal that only has what you would say around lots of people for your family to hear and see anyway? I hate talking to family at holidays, why the fuck would I want to recount my day that would be acceptable to *them*?
    I think my aunt Burnadete is a fucking manipulative selfish bitch. And I think that sexbomb Diana's boyfriend is a stupid fucking loser assclown. And I think my parents are pretty good n cool overall
    There I said it, but sure as hell not going to tell any ofthem that. give me 30 years or a 30 pack and then maybe.

    In some fucked up way I like all the crazy fuckers that come into the coffeeshop as freaked out as it is sometiems. wierd
    And I like playing around and hitting on Diana, in the same sort of way that I like skinamax knowing it won't go anywhere. But I feel bad sometimes because of how often her ass or whatever is brought into a conversation but I enjoy getting paid to see it all, but I don't

want her to think that I only care about her looks but I don't know how to talk to her about other stuff. But I don't really know anything else about her besides the fact that she hot and has lived here for five years is wicked smart has a couple brother and sisters and has a pisspoor boyfriend.

Sogotta love this personal ptuer thing. And gotta love hiddenfoldering and shit. I'd be a perv if I carried a playboy in my bag, but if I'm typing a paper for class with a gig of porn courtesy of Taz a partionclick away, that ok, cause it looks ok cause I'm "working" Too bad I can't get online

Love that they gave this thing to me and that they're "protecting me" from the evil eboogieman with no internet portal. ooooooo

Flashdrive filestransfer, you're my hero. ☺ oooo…real smileyfaces on this shit! riiiight on.

No more risking rents finding saved sexy sessions with online girlys. God I miss those thou, fucking computer crashing virus finding brother. That's the little fucker you need to be keeping your eye on! Well at leats theres nothing stopping me now! Emailing and flashing sexy e-ness to yourself? yes its going ot be a good summer. Oo, let the summer eflirtin begin…

Oh simon, you bad bad boy :☺

Subj:	**Re: WTF?**
Date:	Mon. 5/17/2004 8:49:05 AM EST
From:	theigal@everydaysanctuary.net
To:	ssspellman@everydaysanctuary.net

No problem kid, hope you're alright…just remember I give you what you want.

Well, within consideration. :)

Time to go see the boss. The one that reminds me of the fucking stupid secretary from Office Space.

See…it could be worse

later gator,
Tracy

>>>>
>
>
>
>

Subj:	**Re: WTF?**
Date:	Sat. 5/15/2004 7:12:05 PM EST
From:	ssspellman@everydaysanctuary.net
To:	theigal@everydaysanctuary.net

fuck…

dont kno what to say…think that is enough brutal for now, thanks

>>>>
>
>

>

Subj:	**WTF?**
Date:	Sat. 5/15/2004 9:50:38 AM EST
From:	theigal@everydaysanctuary.net
To:	ssspellman@everydaysanctuary.net

Hunny, you sound so sad.

If I could I would squeeze through the phoneline and give you a big hug. But I can't, so deal with it :)
I am slightly amused though, didn't really know what I was reading for a minute...never received someone's ranting email to themselves. You realize you are a bit mad? Especially because it seems that this "WTF" thing of yours is becoming a habit...take four?
Its lovely to see though, and I'm happy you wrote, you give me a momentary escape...because I'm at work, and keep in mind its Saturday AM. Don't be in too much of a rush to leave your WTF HS times, more extreme but less intense than the WTF mid20s I must say...
Ok, prepare yourself...brutally honest you said?...

Ok I'll tell you straight off, you have no clue what you want right now, so you'd be libel to screw things up with 'that' girl, whenever that girl shows up.
You'll realize in a few years that the people you value now, and I don't mean the ones you want to hang out with all the time, but the ones that are valued, that matter, that if you don't see them for six months are still fresh when you think of them, those are the people who have their heart to share with you and want to know yours...and they ones that are sexy as hell when you figure out what you want and get past your bullshit.
And it is bullshit.
When you figure out what you want, you're figuring out what you want on the inside. You're acting like you know more than everyone else and you're immune. But you chase tits and ass no less than anyone else you fucking horny little boy.
But you are trying to figure it out, and that is encouraging, that's whyI'm even spending time writing this. It's encouraging you use your mind periodically, even if in WTF ways, in between all the clown

dressing, chemical consuming, unintelligible babbling shittalking that I can only imagine is you every other day of the week at school.
So...keep it up and go with it, and you won't still be a horny little boy in old man clothes twenty years from now. And know I'm saying this flat out cause I know it won't seep in if I sugarcoat it. Shit I can't sugarcoat things with all the shit you're around. maybe I should lace it with some narcotic, and then cut it down with some sort of household cleaner, then it might be right. How's that? Perhaps I could order you some sort of online Rx you could OD on as you read this...I hear the Canandians are out to get us like that...no? oh well...
Damn, I thought weed and the occasional odd powder were good enough a few years ago. Times are a changing...Anyway...

What is that phrase, I kid because I care? ;) ok, anyway...'that' girl you want, The girl, is not for you...right now. You know I love you, so I won't hurt you, but I have to say it flat out, you are clueless, and since you don't appreciate or value them, that is why you shouldn't get them.
But inevitably you will hook up with a few, feelings will be hurt, friendships will be lost, because, they are kinds of girls that peak your interest and that you should wait on until you respect them and not just some of their body parts. You're going into it seeing them no better than the highly attractive but utterly worst girls that they struggle to not be but envy for the ease that they can get guys. Your head turns at anyone you find attractive, and in the end, if you are truly one of the nice guys, you will get burned in favor of the asshole guys by a lot of girls and you'll learn to stop popping your tent for all the tits, and get to where you still like boobs, but can start appreciating the breasts of the right good girls. Can you see where I'm going with that one? Can you still connect the dots?
But anyway, try as you might, that won't happen for a while. Just accept it. Partly because here's a newsflash... You're all teenagers and have no fucking clue what you're doing...But you all do such a good job of putting on this act that you know your shit. Its impressive actually how much time and attention goes to it (trust me, I know) Those girls as just as clueless of you, and are scared about opening up so they selfdescruct the chances with the nice guys. And you'll hurt the nice girls in the same way. Basically try to remove those bullshit fairytale lies between romance and friendship. If you can find yourself around people who become good friends and who are attractive, then you are a few steps ahead of all the TV soapopera people.
And one last thing. After having brought up asshole guys and bitch girls, I must say, nearly every girl is a nice girl, and most guys are not bad inside. The question is, is she able to come out of it that way, without getting the shit kicked out of her every time that part peeks out. And as a guy are you going to be able to keep what makes you special

out there and available through all the attemps to be approvable by the 'boys' It's a tough game.
But just be careful not to turn into the fucking fool just to stop getting knocked around while you're down.
Good luck kid.

Let me know if you need any more brutally honest anytime soon, especially if its during business hours...which apparently is any day of the week now.

And hey, have you considered emailing that to Jenn? I know you said that she has herself a boyfriend but still, she'd probably appreciate knowing you value knowing her like that.

Love,
Trace

>>>>
>
>
>
>

Subj:	**Fwd: WTF take four**
Date:	Sat. 5/15/2004 2:34:48 AM EST
From:	ssspellman@everydaysanctuary.net
To:	theigal@everydaysanctuary.net

Here it is, cant believe im sending something like this to you. tell me what your brutal is thou, whatcha think?

si

>>>>
>
>
>

>

Subj:	**WTF take four**
Date:	Mon. 5/10/2004 2:08:02 AM EST
From:	ssspellman@everydaysanctuary.net
To:	ssspellman@everydaysanctuary.net

shocking…its time for another WTF…

but seriously, what the fuck? I mean really WHAT THE FUCK? Is there some law dat says that two people both cant like each other, otherwise we all fuckign blow up? Cause yet again superhotcool girl says she valudes my 'friendship' too much to risk losing it. 'I like you like a brother' funny y is that what they say right before never talking to you agian. Ooooooh, so that kind of friend? riiiight.
Y doesnt anyone want me? Angie sure did before we started flirtni and talking…and then boom. Never changes I cant say this to any of the guys, its all about hooking up and shit…but it never goes beyond names dates and places. Why cant I have someone I can talk to like Jenn, but who wants my shit like that Jersey chick or, i dunno? is that too much to ask? what really pisses me off is watching all the guys i know fuck it up with the cool girls…y?? how? what the hell was wrong with them, they want to hang out with your friends, can talk about things past the stupid shit, arnt crying and wining in your ear every othr hour, and actually have some sort of hope gting out of this fucking town and besides the fact theyr hot and want to get on you Mad props to them! Yeaaa, but no were looking for bitches I'm sorry. just wrong isnt it? Fucking fools. I know when I get a girl like that, I'm not going to fuck it up goddamnit

Fucking fools.

Subj:	**Re: no subject**
Date:	Mon. 5/17/2004 9:34:01 AM EST
From:	theigal@everydaysanctuary.net
To:	ssspellman@everydaysanctuary.net

I'm so proud of you for going down there!! Trust me, that'll be something cool to look back on in a few years and know you saw...let alone took part in. And those are some good stories!
Good luck with the scamming

Will write more soon, promise :)

love,
trace

>>>>
>
>
>
>

Subj:	**no subject**
Date:	Mon. 5/17/2004 3:08:52 AM EST
From:	ssspellman@everydaysanctuary.net
To:	theigal@everydaysanctuary.net

Yo Trace!!

Dude, seriously. I don't know what to make of it all.

Was such a fucking smooth day, but so strange though too

So that dude I met at work a couple weeks ago ashad came into down again, and I guess came into town and said he saw me in the window and wanted to know what I was doing after work cause he bussed it into town for the weekend and was meeting some Brandeis friends and they were all going downtown or something to hang out for the afternoon after they were done with Waltham.(would only take two

seconds for me) but anyway, so it was rad since I was just getting off, said sure if they could wait like twenty minutes since I was finishing up the buttcrack am shift.
So we go down to Newbury and mess around for a bit. dude that indy coffee shop down there is so rad! I didn't find out where they all knew each other from but they all go dancing a lot or somethin…and in the end I find out that they all got together to go to that gay marriage shit that was going down. It was only then I figured the shit out.
So we hung out for a few and then they said they were going to some coffeeshop in Davis Sq so I all I told them I'd head back with them there on the Red and take the comm. rail back to Wal and shit, not really feeling coo with the idea of being dependent on a bunch of gay guys for a midnight ride home or somethign. But somehow he convinced me to stay saying it was allgood , so all of a sudden I'm calling up my stepmom to check in and that I was in Harvard Sq cause I needed to 'research' for that project in science at their library cause the shit wasn't in school, Dude…she bought it. I guess if I lie about doing work its beyond question?? Anyway, told her I was doing that and then taking the commuter rail back to someones house near Bran for the gp meeting. And so anyway, we end up going to Diesel Cafe. That place is so fuckin cool btw, like a garage with all the tools and shit on the walls, wifi people everywhere, makes me wish I had myself all set like that to, anyway, so we hang out there and chat, pretty cool kids actually, all first years at Am or Bran except ashad, and it was so strange…I didn't feel strange around them. How does that work? It feels weird that it didn't'? Anyway, Ashad joked about me being out of my element, and it being all cute…I told no and tol him to fuck off … and he was like yea yea, then why not come with us to the city hall tonight, and I was like well maybe I will. Really bad bluff.
LSS we end up leaving somewhere near midnight to somewhere on Mass Ave wherever it was, and it was fucking crazy. The fucking street was shut down. So we had to park in BFE and walk over and the street and the hill in front of the building were all covered with people. Was way weird. But after it all I have to admit, it wasn't all that bad. like last week there was apoll and I was all for the marriage amendment shit, but now I dont know, wasn't that big a deal. The supporter people had such a cool vibe to em all laughing and friendly

Fucked up having heard all the shit about how this whole thing is so fucked up and all and then seeing what was really FUCKED was the fucking protesters. The only people out there protesting were FUCKING CRAZY. Dude they were holding signs saying that fags caused the space shuttle to crash and shitlike that. What? But the worst one, I won't ever forget it…and I shit you not: "Thank God for Sept 11th" … WHAT??????????? Apcoloptic freaks…anyway so we end up on the hill around shit loads of people, (have to say tho, I couldnt figure out a few of them, … guy/girl/misc) :) but it felt so cool there odd enough…college kids from allaround there making fun of the fuckers across the street, but then the cops show up in riot gear and we all start getting anxious wwith the WTF is romney up too (guess he was trying to rewrite laws or reading em different or something? but they shove everybody out of the way on the steps going up to the building and just stand there. Was fucking crazy…riot gear cops making sure the path was clear? and then I guess couples started going up, and it was freaking strange seeing sets of old guys or chicks walking up there, but the crowd was rad, all singing love songs and beattles songs and sometimes fruity cheesy showtunes and then stopping to applaude people going up the steps. Some of em were freaking old!! So weird. Beattles songs, cops proecting love, Jesus namedroppers supporting 9/11?!? Anyway. The coolest thing though I thought was when the crowd started singing the national anthem and the starspangled banner and shit, was so cool hearing that from that group against the protesters across the street with their crazy ass signs. Some of the songs were kinda fucked up though I thought, trying to talk about unity and then there was that song about from this city to that or from that mountain to the ocean this is America and shit, sounded like that manifest destiny shit we had to learn in history…so they're all singing about love and shit but had to piss on the america indians and shit. But they were def cooler than the psychos across the street. Johns dad went off about the fags and shit the other day at the deli and I thought he had a point, but then when you see this kind of shit you see the REAL freaks, the Kansas hick ones that say God mailed them their signs and told them to come to Mass (seriously, this guy Vick we were standing near had his laptop with him I don't know why, but he pulled it out when everyone was laughing at the crazies, their manifesto or whatever was all like the devil is the one issueing these marriages and shit. Ok, so God and the devil are all postal now? Why the hell can't they get with the E-shit and massemail us all if they have something

to say, why always go through these freaky fucks? Anyway, that guy Vick was funny as hell. Hypergay def, but funny as hell. He started introducing me around to the friends he was around, "hey soandso, this is Simon. He's straight" So fucking weird being referred like that. But anyway, so he was like a total Indian (India Indian and was going around joking he should be able to be the first winner of the greencard via gay marriage sweepstakes just for fun and shit cause I guess he isn't perm res. And then he all goes no I couldn't get it, since I'm brown! I was like what?!? and he just said he's happy being brown and all but that sometimes it'd be nice to able to be a full commonwealther...guess he was saying that if he was an aussie or kiwi he wouldn't have had as much problem but he was from the brown part of the commonwealth which of course gave him and ashad loads to talkabout since Ashad is arab but is british or something cant remember exactly. Thought that was funny as fuck. takin an English test to get in to the US even though its his first lang. So yea it was right after that tha ashad came back over from someplace and they met, funny as fuck. they went back and forth talking about that sorta shit, with the whole brown commonwealth sorta shit . So anywaythat totally killed all the oddness to it all, all of a sudden nothing was black or white or gay or straight, more like misc and brown :) so yea then just normal people bullshit, and lots of love walking up the stairs. Funny, they were all laughing, saying shit like, "love closed down Mass Ave!" so anyway the crazies across the street left right after midnight cause they had to get up early in the am or somethignto go to Boston cityhall or some shit with their stupidass signs. I'm sorry, their stupidass 'holy' signs.
Anyway, those were all somerad crazy kids tho.

Anyway, gotta crash, copped out of class tomorrow, parents were cool with it as long as was willing to trade off with extra hours at the cafe after I wake up...just need to keep my stories straight and I got a nice little scam going 0;)

Jittery smiles from the wicked am
simon

Dude, forgot, the funniest thing about last night...after a bunch of couples had come out with the lisecences two chicks came out but one was wearing a leather jacket and was all like football player body and stopped and opened up her jacket laughing to show her boobs to

the crowd to show her chickness, you would have loved it, was funny as hell! Fucking crowd loved it
And then this press photographer guy comes out to send his images and shows some of us what was all hapening inside with dig pics and there was the classic pic of the couple cake thing but 2 big ol nicely suited dudes caking each other. Was actually so cute!

notice I had a bit of coffee tonight?

anyway, if I get any sleep I'll probably dream of coffee and cakes with two guys on it…
well, no actually I'll go for the two girls instead….yeaaaa ;)

Subj:	**Taz IM 5-17**
Date:	Mon. 5/17/2004 10:14:32 PM EST
From:	ssspellman@everydaysanctuary.net
To:	ssspellman@everydaysanctuary.net

DevilLAX35: dude what happened 2u last night
castaspell: whats up
castaspell: went to study at Bran with a famfriend, hitched a ride on their van at the shop after got off
DevilLAX35: your such a tool
DevilLAX35: we were all over at kevins drinkin playin poker and shit all nite wit his rents outa town, u missed out
DevilLAX35: and speaking of where the fuck were u 2day
castaspell: lay off dicknuts, got home late, convinced my rents to signoff on an offday since there wasn't shit going on in class and got home late from studying, they went for it as long as i went into the shop to ask bout pickin up some hours this summer after I woke up, just got home, and my cell is dead cause I lost the charger
DevilLAX35: ok ok, dont go get ur pantys in a bunch
castaspell: yea yea. so que pasa with you
DevilLAX35: just chillin, went to see spider2 with some peeps
castaspell: you cock, thanks for the invite. how was it?
DevilLAX35: was alright, the stunts kick ass and the chick was hott
castaspell: right on, yea I'd me all over her
DevilLAX35: ya think
castaspell: its too bad movies now aren't they used to be before like in the 80s or whatever, u know, withh the two sec of TnA. Whats with this wet tshirt spiderman scene in the first and and temp island bullshit but then janet and howard stern get stoned for straight out showing it or saying it
DevilLAX35: no doubt
DevilLAX35: like for us, its okay to screw a hs chick, but u cant take those good pics of her, u can take pics of her in a bikini and underwear and shit but its bad if u can c a nip, what the fuck
DevilLAX35: fucking fags allowd to get married but we cant go down the street go to a stripculb

castaspell: yea I hear ya on those pics, thatll be cool next year huh
castaspell: that gay marriage shit doesn't bug me tat much
DevilLAX35: what od u mean, u going soft
castaspell: nah, just mean less of them lookin round to scoreif theyre married right?
DevilLAX35: yea i guess so but its fucked up with the hole social acceptance shit
DevilLAX35: whats next
DevilLAX35: i heard the next thing theyl do is start demanding more gay judges and cops and shit like queer aff action demanding special rights and shit
DevilLAX35: think about how fuckd up it be if like 30% of teachers had to be gay or if fag couples tookove homecoming and shit and all the songs were all lezrock and shit and all the machines in school had to go to all that soy and fruity shit
castaspell: yea I gues that would be messed up but all that shit cant' happen andits not like they all listen to that shit or drink that shit: still don't know about that soy shit though…
castaspell: diana was tryingto get me to try it the other day at the shop, I was all like lewis black going, soy milk? wheres the fucking tit if its milk
DevilLAX35: who
castaspell: Diana, the short hispanic chick at the shop
DevilLAX35: nah the dude, whos the dude
castaspell: oh, you know the fucking strokecase guy on the daily show, the one that just goes off on something every day?
DevilLAX35: oh yea hes fuking cool
castaspell: yea, that was from some special, went off on that and all the fucking bottle water bullshit
DevilLAX35: yea no kidding, what the fuck
DevilLAX35: buy a fucking sports bottle and be done with it
castaspell: exactly
castaspell: theres people that come into the shop almost everyday for fuckign water, and then don't even leave their fucking change in the jar. 18 cents. 18 fucking cents! Fuck you, you pay nearly 2 bucks for water a day and you take your 18 fucking cents. Cheap ass fuckers.
DevilLAX35: yea thats twisted
DevilLAX35: how much u make on tips aday

castaspell: depends morn shifts r good I guess so I'm looking forward to summer
castaspell: the nights suck why i go for aftersch
castaspell: like 20 or 25 each if a couple there, mostly its peoples change so depends on how busy itis
DevilLAX35: if i workedthere id be givin out free cups to all the girlys prolly get fired
castaspell: yea u def would
castaspell: they got cameras and shit ... guess the owners aren't to bad, could be wrose but cant imagine doing this shti past hs
castaspell: was talking to this famfriend last fam bday or whateva, guess she woked in a bar for awhileand did coffee a bit said the thing that sucked about the coffeeshit is that you spend more time making peoples drinks than at a bar and they don't fucking tip as mch as at a bar...
DevilLAX35: never thought bout that, that is fucked up
DevilLAX35: im not about to fucking drop a dollar tip 4 my buck and change cup of brew thou
castaspell: oh no, but I'm talking about those fucking people with their I want a large this with that but only half of this and two shot of that and some sprinkles of this but with only a piunch of this and then wait no can you take off the sprinkles and add foam and oooh wait whip crema too. So its like five minutes later you get it to them, that'l be 4.75, they don't even have there money ready and then finally fucking pull out a five and MAYBE leave the fucking quarter.
castaspell: them and the fucking water fuckers
DevilLAX35: thats weak
DevilLAX35: dude spell, u should tell them to fuckoff with the pussy order and tell em ull just make the shit up and to just deal
castaspell: lol
castaspell: yea I wish
castaspell: be cool though
DevilLAX35: def
DevilLAX35: be like... ull get ur coffee when I get a gw in the tipjar, next...
castaspell: right on!
castaspell: yea i should use that one someday
DevilLAX35: so fuckface u gonna ballup and showup 2morrow
castaspell: yea if mood suits me
castaspell: I'll find a fortune cookie and ask it if I should

DevilLAX35: haha not fucking difficult on that fucking street
DevilLAX35: alright playa, later
castaspell: later

Subj:	**Kristi IM 5-20 sexyyy**
Date:	Thr. 5/20/2004 11:30:12 PM EST
From:	ssspellman@everydaysanctuary.net
To:	ssspellman@everydaysanctuary.net

HoTBodBaBy02: Hey there hotstuff
castaspell: Hey sexy!! long time no talk!!! what are you doing?
HoTBodBaBy02: Nothin jus chillin gettign ready 4 bed... steve just drove me home, was babysitting 2nite
HoTBodBaBy02: what about you?
castaspell: I'm been chilling here, no HW so been doing some cds for someone. would someone with a bday coming up want a cd to? :)
HoTBodBaBy02: only if you wanna make me one
HoTBodBaBy02: O;)
castaspell: What would you like it to be, I don't know what you need/want...:) hard to tho cause lost most of my mp3s cause of the fucking borther.
HoTBodBaBy02: LoL
HoTBodBaBy02: well what do you have to satisfy me....hmmmm...
castaspell: Hmm, I don't know how...
castaspell: Should I surprise you with some sweet you are so beautiful songs, and some fun songs etc?
HoTBodBaBy02: how bout a couple your so hot and I want you songs to ;)
castaspell: ummm...damn, that sounds a little too good
castaspell: I'll do my best
HotBodBaBy02: I'd like to feel what your best is like someday
castaspell: 0;) DAMN!!
castaspell: And they will be so accurate. Why do you always have to have a boyfriend whenever we get to chat like this?
castaspell: OK, wow.
HoTBodBaBy02: was teased a bit of you from that homecoming story with that girl... dancing to Justin song

HoTBodBaBy02: ok stop thinking about that, don't wanna be gettin horny now
HoTBodBaBy02: ummm.........nevermind, not thinking bout it anymore, shut up kristi
castaspell: You are SO BAD! Why do you do this to me!
HoTBodBaBy02: heehee
HoTBodBaBy02: yes surprise me with some sexy songs!!!!!!!!!!! O;)
HoTBodBaBy02: but make sure you have that Justin song on it! So you can tease me back :)
castaspell: Def! So I can make you randy?
castaspell: ok
HoTBodBaBy02: Oh yeah i can gte off just by looking at your picture
HoTBodBaBy02: (why i had to take it out of my locker at skool) ;)
castaspell: Oh really???
HoTBodBaBy02: Oh yes and because all the girls were droolin on it
HoTBodBaBy02: heehee
castaspell: Don't give me to big of a head.
HoTBodBaBy02: LoL
HoTBodBaBy02: hahaha
HoTBodBaBy02: i wish you couldve come up for the holidays
HoTBodBaBy02: ;(
HoTBodBaBy02: or anytime
castaspell: Me too...it sucks, I hope I can before graduation.
HoTBodBaBy02: ;)
HoTBodBaBy02: dont get my hopes up
HoTBodBaBy02: i miss talking to you
castaspell: Well in a year or two maybe I will have the perks to come for your graudation
HoTBodBaBy02: Ill be 17!!!!!!!!!!!
HoTBodBaBy02: wait! almost 18

HoTBodBaBy02: u should wait until the summer then, then we can go really crazy. hinthint
castaspell: OMG!!!!!
HoTBodBaBy02: cant wait
castaspell: :) Yea I can't wat to see us then, scary a little bit though...I will like it when all of a sudden I'm not lusting over anyone illegal in a couple years. Icouldn't imagine wanting someone in my stepbros grade, couldn't believe you were in it
HoTBodBaBy02: it will be so fun..... hopefully ill be able to save enough for a trip out there! ;) i couldn't believe someone so cute and older would want to talk to me just to talk to me
HoTBodBaBy02: LoL
HoTBodBaBy02: and stuff like that yah know
castaspell: Yea, I can't wait see you out this way someday.
castaspell: Well sexy chick in pajamas thinking about dirty dancing after a graduation, I need to do some french homework...maybe i'll just make up sentences of all the things I want to do to you...oo...I mean with you....I mean together...:)
HoTBodBaBy02: hahaha ok... your something teasing me like tht! hahaha
HoTBodBaBy02: my mind is too active
HoTBodBaBy02: Ill talk to you later k sweetie... miss you want you.... Opps!
castaspell: Well take that mind and imagine taking my active hands over your body so that I can slip a article of clothing here or there to see what the webcam couldn't show
HoTBodBaBy02: ummm... ok thats enough
HoTBodBaBy02: you got me wiht the active hands
castaspell: Oh, where are your hands traveling?
HoTBodBaBy02: oh theyr just taking a trip
HoTBodBaBy02: down south
HoTBodBaBy02: LoL
castaspell: Hmm...:) where is that exactly, the south is a large region, what country down south? is it humid down there?
HoTBodBaBy02: im going to bed now but not to go sleep yet

HoTBodBaBy02: LOL
HoTBodBaBy02: Their on their way to Vaginistan
HoTBodBaBy02: LOL
HoTBodBaBy02: Heeheehee
castaspell: Well…what if I told you thinking about your hands traveling makes mine wnat to take a trip. :) (or that they were already doing little recon missions for the last few min) Oh really? I like that country, I visit it as often as the offcials allow me to. Too bad there is no access to your lands right now.
HoTBodBaBy02: LOL
HoTBodBaBy02: well mines always open to an older boy from far faraway who wants to dance me round all sexy and has equl thoughts.
HoTBodBaBy02: just remember that
HoTBodBaBy02: but i must go to bed
castaspell: I can't believe you are doing that, after those itmes we discussed shit like that. :) Oh really? I like an open border policy, are there lots of tours that I can take?
HoTBodBaBy02: yeah well there is a warm bed waitin for you to get your ass out here
castaspell: Ok,I'll fantasize about my dream trip to your beautiful neighborhood in Vaginistan …great climate, great personality. :)
castaspell: I will when I can.
castaspell: I'd like to be a permanent resident of your region. I'd like to be the perm Vaginistani ambassador :)
HoTBodBaBy02: :O)
HoTBodBaBy02: it would be a pleasure tohave you
HoTBodBaBy02: But i really have to go, since im a god litlte skool girl
castaspell: Good to kno.. :) take care cutie yes you are ;)
HoTBodBaBy02: dreamin bout you nitenite

Subj:	**Re: silly Simon**
Date:	Sat. 5/22/2004 11:49:54 AM EST
From:	shamelesssavant@everydaysanctuary.net
To:	ssspellman@everydaysanctuary.net

Sorry, no off, guess I can understand that thou
I've never had anyone explain any of that to me before.
That's really fucked up it was like only 40 years ago with the CR shit yea, didn't exactly shine birhgt in my hist class coupe years ago...and I mean our hist teach pretty much just gave up after 1900 with how bad we were...

Teach me some shit thou whats up with this ICU shit?

Sim

And its not my parents...a dad and a stepmom (shit back from elem schyears...long story

>>>
>
>
>
>

Subj:	**Re: silly Simon**
Date:	Thr. 5/20/2004 9:40:03 AM EST
From:	ssspellman@everydaysanctuary.net
To:	ssspellman@everydaysanctuary.net

Whats the big deal? What is the big fucking deal? With your background and you ask me that.
Simon, It was only 40 years ago with the Civil Rights Bill finally making all that fucked up overt race discrimination illegal...you're parents grew up in a country where it was still acceptable to go

separate but equal. And now you have to ask me what the big deal is with all the things going on now?
This is no different.
I don't need a legal contract to say I love my husband, But I do need a legal setup to allow me to be at his bedside if he was in intensive care or vise versa.
An attending nurse denying a perswon access for lack of that legal standing is no different than someone denying care to someone a hundred years ago based on their skin color. I'm sorry, you can't come into this hospital, whites only.
Not that its much better here now with insurance as it is. Yea health care is a human right here, as long as you can afford it.

And you have the audacity to ask me what is the big deal?
Separate but equal is the big deal. Didn't work then, won't work now. One groups resistance to change or termporay discomfort over another groups rights, or health, or education?
I always say I'll be damned before I let anyone control my destiny in that way.
But then a simple twist of fate and boom, that's exactly where youre at and what's happening, some desk clerk decides my fate, not my soulmate.

Simple as that.

Ashad

>>>>
>
>
>
>

Subj:	**Re: silly Simon**
Date:	Thr. 5/20/2004 6:08:21 AM EST
From:	ssspellman@everydaysanctuary.net
To:	shamelesssavant@everydaysanctuary.net

Yea things are crazy busy here too. What the hells there left to do? I just dont see what the big fucking deal is, its all going on now and it was cool being there and seeing them all cool and happy, what aer you getting your panties in a bunch for now with it happenin? I mean you say you dont care about whether you marry someone if you love them so why all the fuss, its summer for you already shit I'd be out partying and relaxing. What are you up to all summer anyway?

Sim

>>>>
>
>
>
>

Subj:	**silly Simon**
Date:	Wed. 5/19/2004 10:12:40 AM EST
From:	shamelesssavant@everydaysanctuary.net
To:	ssspellman@everydaysanctuary.net

    Finally able to email you. Was a great weekend all around. I won't definitely be against it in the future.

    After our weekend and Monday in Cambridge and Boston me and my mates have been trying to get through the rest of our exams and move out and in and whatnot. I'm still in the process of packing up for the move for the summer into the flat of my friend Erin in Northhampton next week and helping out with more HRC projects as the amendment vote nears.

    Hope you're week went well and you didn't get in the shits from your cool weekend with wonderful people. :)

Cheers and best regards,

Ashad

Subj:	**Re: why cant nasa chicks be like in startrek**
Date:	Mon. 5/24/2004 6:32:10 PM EST
From:	NateDogg814@everydaysanctuary.net
To:	"Simon" ssspellman@everydaysanctuary.net

No doubt on that titlin shit!!!
So cuz, whats up with in your biznas?

Hey seriously slime, you don't have to settled for the fucjking stupid chicks. Nancy is all smart and shit and its cool. Especially sicne she does my math homework smtimes. ;) just takes some chocolate and massaging. but seriously she doesnt have that stupid ass attitude pricness bullshit your always complaining bout, go for some smarties. There b some hella hot brains out tha let me tell ya.

totally know what you mean mtho about the science shit!! that is so wack that we both were doing the total lazyass thing with the same show shit. think we must have the same sat thing or something. was checking that shit out myself the other day bored as fuck. the female astronomer epople on that shit could be be lqqkers too. like weather chicks. They could kcik the wether chicks asses with

their graphics and videos and shit. citycams vs saturn flybys? no comp they just need to spend more time on appearance thou than the weather chicks and then some on their stage prescence   altho out here theyd have to compete with daily highspeed chases on the bodycountnews.
That would be awesome, turn on nasa for hot smart chicks that got some lownekc tops and talk about insertion and shit   lol
man nasa could be the hottest thing since discovering the secrets of the sex isle in the bookstore, remember that?? I had a kickass sci teacher when all that shit went down with the mars bullshit.you know what im talking bout right? Who the fuck has a 100million dollar ooops with math. oops, a littlee off course, maybe they should pad their budget allowing for one of those per year, just incase or something. with jon stewart right now thou, wow…you found dirt in those rings. no shit? wow. Can I have a millions dollars to build something to go find penguin shit in antarctica? Thatd be greaaat.
oh shit!!   sobookstore. give you the vicarious thing.   so me and nanc…yea, we were all like in a movie scene or something, going back and forth with this KamSu sex book in the store like, well lets try that shit on page 46, and how bout 32 too. Was so fucking amazing! You need to get a girlfriend si, seriously you dnot realize what your missing out on when youcan get hella creative and siht.
If I can ever get her cloned or I,Roboted,(doesn't that shit lqqk tight??) ill send you the betamodel to test out coo?

And its lame here sometimes thou too, where you hit up out there/ like what clubs and shit? whats the dealio for you this summer? My bio is work and riding. A new skate park near my hood'll will get its regular luvin from me and my wheels this sum. the coast life is cool whenyou can get nerait, but sucks otherwise…about as bad out here as the isolation of burbs there, the real fucking OC baby, the fucking like a superbig whatever it is you said was ristsy NewburySt or whatever planted on Gitmo. Isolated as fuck and only really cool if you got yourself some serious green or are packed out with your forties and the fortwine.

Anyway brotha, gotta go get my chem groove on before the gf shows up or else ill get a little lecture. Not the kind of lip I'm looking for, you kno this

hasta
Nate

>>>>
>
>
>
>

Subj:	**Why cant nasa chicks be like in startrek**
Date:	Sun. 5/23/2004 1:42:35 PM EST
From:	ssspellman@everydaysanctuary.net
To:	NateDogg814@everydaysanctuary.net

Dude, know what you mean, its amazing how much stuff is in these movies than I never realized. We grew up always complaining about the fucking shallowstories and shti, but there are some movie people out there that are the movie versions of the ClancyChriton clan huh with the research enough into it your getting a little eductainmention as well. You remember the first time you heard about the whole matrix shit?

And you go around thinking, "its like so cool how the matrix can be watched on so many levels." We're so fucking brainnumbed the fact that we realized this way after. You ever seen Contact? I thought the movie was such shit a few years ago when my parents made me go as a kid. Remember thinking it was so fucking boring and stupid, since I was like 10 at the time and was all like, whatever the aliens her dad and shit...oh fuck, my bad if I just ruined it. but if you haven't seen it check it out if even just for the starting scene, it does that whole factor of 10 shit from like basic freshman science, its fucking incredible how tiny you feel all of a sudden but then with being able to see it all you feel all big and special too, which I guess wsa the whole message of the story but anyway, its so much better after having learned about some of that shit in school and can enjoy the shows more that its actually not sciencefiction. Star Trek is still lame with all that imaginary perfect world bullshit but its not like we don't all have our personal fucking tricorders now you know...all taking pictures and sending em to people and playing tetris on the T (subway) and all. Anyway, so yea just fucking crazy that way.
Was flipping channels the other night unable to sleep from the lateshift at the shop and for the fucksake of it I checked out the nasa channel. They really should get some makeup artists on those fucking Saturn picture people who can't seem to find a mall that is within a decade of fashionable. Shit with the CGI getting going on, as cool as Saturn is they have to eb competing with Riddick and all. I mean Saturn is real and all. But lucas can kick their asses with just a few days work with Naboo :)

god I need a girlfriend. Soon ill probably sink to joining the fucking geek clubs afterschool and goin for science and math girls. Arrrrrg. As it is Im thinking of skippin out on the team this fall, my bodys still messed up from Feb. Fuck I need to get out of this fcking town. Whats it like there? Cool shit to do wenever you want I bet. This sucks, all the cool places are so far away might as well be in FL, am able to get out that way about as often as we visit down there.

Subj:	**Re: dirty little boy**
Date:	Thr. 6/03/2004 11:32:02 PM EST
From:	ssspellman@everydaysanctuary.net
To:	Angiepangie@everydaysanctuary.net

    Um, straight off...I have never had, nor will I ever intend to ever bring up your feminine hygiene products in a conversation, especially in a manner of a information request. Hmm, in fact you were the first person to bring that up, just likethe boobs :) Hope the boob topic wasn't to off the odd end...that is cool you are cool with yourself...if it makes any difference, up until a few months ago I didn't know anyone like that, and now a couple friends in one way or another have hinted to that, and I never could tell, and if you told me and made me choose I bet I wouldn't be able to...want to find out? ;) jk well we are all diff right? speaking of right that is the opposite of my directional angle to the world...its a two way street now isn't it? bet you really wantedto know that huh that I pull a clinton and wont huant your dreams or anything to bad I cant get nothing for having it public knowledge tho well I'm trying to finish pu a paper tonight, a few hours of working on it would help, but I can't make myself do it. After that, time to work on french, which I'm barely passing so I won't coninue on in that...and otherwise just waiting for finals...I'll be done on next week...what about you? I'm still just digging this computer I just scored though! Did I tell you bout it?? My dad got a new laptop from work and so they passovered this to me. (they took out the modem and shit though, wanting to still regulate my behavior with the naught-Estuff. It rocks you help me out in that realm ;) Angie with her hyperlinks, what more do you need? ;)

    So you enjoy emails from me? happy to hear, caues I get excited when I get the pleasure of having you in my box...:;) And then you send me funny porn links, you are fucking awesome man! I love you man! No you can't have my budlight, go get your own. Dude, why'd you have to move all across state lines and shit? Although if I had to see you tomorrow I prolly would have trouble with the eye contact, better having some time to let the information settle. You should transfer to a uni round here so I can come party with you and you can hook me up with your hot friends. Sorry, I'm a little weird right now due to a few injections of coffee and now with a mind on porn and your boobs....oops, my bad.

Well at least it wasn't a request for further information right? ;)

dumbass simon

>>>>
>
>
>

Subj:	**dirty little boy**
Date:	Tue. 6/01/2004 8:14:22 PM EST
From:	Angiepangie@everydaysanctuary.net
To:	ssspellman@everydaysanctuary.net

     What's up kid? I am enjoying an early evening off from work and I finished the amount of studying that I had assigned myself to do tonight ...... so basically I'm in one of those few moments of bliss. Good luck on all your finals.....they suck but once your finished, the summer is going to be awesome right? seriously, simon...summer classes...just say no! be happy you're not doing it too...but im cool with this after july is over ill be able ot take off for a study aboard next spring. So you going anywhere special this summer? I might be heading to Daytona with my friend Rachel whose dad lives down there in august. Ok, so I will answer you this one question, this one time, ok? And only because I have to admit I was the one that brought it up I'll be honest, and prolly only because you are out in Waltham rather than around here. The reason I'm sometimes selfconcious about my body, and thank you for what you said, you're sweet, is that...well I'll say that its hard to find bras that work forme as my breasts refuse to be teamplayers. So you know how some girls complain cause they can't find jeans that work for their butts and their legs at the same time or whatever, yea, trying making a B and an A feel at home in the same bra isnt easy either.   But I've accepted it. So I'm not symmetrical. Cest la vie right? So anyway, I just have to remind myself that the whole world doesn't revolve around boobs, contrary to popular belief. Although maybe that's why I got the eyebrow pieced on that side, to make up for my substandard boob. :) Or maybe it just looked better on

that side. Well I suppose there are worse things you could to do try and counteract the imperfections huh.
And so, as long as you don't start quizzing me on feminine hygiene products or where I go when I'm blue, because I just wouldn't want you up and showing up, I think this could still be a beautiful friendship. Good luck with the rest of your shit week :)

    soft smiles,
        ang

Subj:	**Jenn IM 6-6**
Date:	Sun. 6/06/2004 2:45:32 PM EST
From:	ssspellman@everydaysanctuary.net
To:	"Simon" ssspellman@everydaysanctuary.net

castaspell: Hey gorgeous
Jennzen710: Hey hun
Jennzen710: What are you up to?
castaspell: oh, ova at Travs house
castaspell: jenn can I ask you a ?
Jennzen710: Sure, what's up?
castaspell: is there some special fasination girls have with butts that I don't know about?
Jennzen710: What do you mean? liking a guys butt?
castaspell: It was weird, you know that girl I was all telling you about? Well she had this thing with my ass. So we're making out and I'm all going up her shirt and shit like before and its all good and she starts playing around down there only after she lets me start on her, but she doesn't give me a good job, just sort of plays with it for a minute and then is all playing around under my sack and shit.
Jennzen710: Sorry. Don't know what to tell you.
castaspell: I don't get it, I didn't know what to say though, cause I still wanted her to finish me off so I didn't want to piss off, but she just kept doing that even when I got into her and made her get more into it, and then she was all like, she was sorry and felt bad but had to go home and shit.
castaspell: cause it was near her curfew
Jennzen710: Well if she was worried about getting caught by your parents or getting in trouble with hers?

castaspell: well yea, but I just don't get it, I play with her boobs and her box and she play around with my ass...what the fuck? Is she some fucking gay guy trapped in some chicks body?
Jennzen710: I don't know. Ask her about it.
castaspell: I cant do that!
castaspell: I dont know Fuck her.
Jennzen710: OH don't you blow her off just from that Simon. If she is cool as you say does that really matter, is it really worth fucking it up over, maybe she just wants to take it slower. maybe she really likes you
castaspell: Yea I guess
castaspell: anyway, thanks
castaspell: hey I gotta jet
Jennzen710: no prob
castaspell: ttyl
Jennzen710: bye hun

Subj:	**Re: a little help...**
Date:	Mon. 6/07/2004 9:42:10 AM EST
From:	theigal@everydaysanctuary.net
To:	ssspellman@everydaysanctuary.net

    Simon, you really need to remember to have isseues on the weekdays if you want more immediate attention. But I suppose this is forgivable, although you sure as hell know how to distract me from work...I should start waiting til afternoon to read your emails. And then charge you :) jk...I like that you write me for help.

    And...

    You're hopeless...you know this right? But never the less I'll give it a try anyway, to see if we can add 'romantic' to that rather than 'dickmunch' or something like that. Soo...still want me to continue?

    Sim, you know I love you, and I want to help you, but this is hard, because I don't want to divulge secrets and help you hurt girls...so I will help you a bit...but you have to stop being a fucking guy for a moment. OK? I know you're pretty fly for a white guy, but you also can be a total tool like is shown in that video...oh wait, you're a little baby and probably won't get that...how about Malibus Most Wanted sort of tool, ok? Ok, and off we go

    Well I'll tell you straight off, you did find a normal girl.

    But also straight off, she would have no interest in you if she just wanted to get off. Do you really think you know what goes through a girls head to know what they are thinking or feeling? Do you really think you know what you're doing in that regard to be in demand? I've been known to do the same thing she's doing as a matter of fact, and most of the time it was after I had become comfortable with myself, figured out what was going on with the person and how I felt.

How long have you known this girl? Do you know much of anything about her?

She likes spending time with you obviously, and she wants to be close and get physical with you yes, but see, that's not the first thing she's thinking about. I know, I know. But trust me, it is possible. And is likely. She may be new to all of this so keep that squarely in mind. But also either she could be freaked out by penis or jiz as any normal girl is at some point, or maybe she's been around a bit longer and is just freaked out about that coming out of you because of the risk of you going away right afterwards that she would no doubt have experienced from previous boys.

Fuck Sim, you could get yourself off anytime you want, and I don't want to even think about how often that probably is. So whats the big deal if she didn't give you that right then and there? You're a demanding little hormone aren't you? Have you looked at the fact that you are complaining that a girl, who you say is cute, and more importantly, who you say is cool on top of that, wants to make out with you and wants you to hold her and wants to above all, get to know you? Yes. Brutal.

So let me not talk to a teenage boy for a moment and pretend you actually think above your waist for a few seconds, and listen. Girls are different. We don't want you 'to get in our pants,' we want to be with you and we want to share ourselves with you and be able to feel the real you, but only when you are not thinking just about you. See how that works?

Were you really thinking about her, and about what you were doing to her? Or were you just trying to get her to give that to you too? You were just pushing buttons weren't you? Like someone's who's new at mortal combat or whatever it is now...they don't know what they are doing but they know that mashing a bunch of buttons does something and will see if that's good enough.

I'll tell you this, no girl ... no one wants to feel like they're just good enough...you don't need to know exactly what your doing, but simply that you're not just doing something to her, and your not just doing something to her for you, but your doing that to her *for her*.

You need to be thinking about her. And her feelings. (besides your own) Only then are you ever really with that person rather than spending time with them trying to get rewarded. Only when you change it up like that does anything good really come…and cum. It's a benefit, it's a bonus, its not a fucking commodity that you purchase or trade for. She isn't a baseball card. Does that make sense? If you want that, I don't have to tell you all you have to do is spend a few bucks on beer and condoms and get yourself drunk at the sorts of parties I hope you don't make a habit of going to..

    She's scared I bet.

    As long as you're willing to learn and grow, you can get better…but it better not just be an act and on the surface. You better not fucking hurt her, or I'll fucking hurt you…because…

    She feels more than you do. Not saying her feelings are more important than yours, but that she probably has hers out there more often and risks more. She was mashing buttons on you too I bet, scared though to use the buttons she knows would work for *that*, because she probably likes being with you and that fucking freaks her out! Because she doesn't want to be dependent on anyone for that feeling. But that feeling is amazing. And if you ever stop thinking with your secondary brain, and remember, it is secondary, you'll start to understand that. It's fun for you when you have someone else get you off huh? But you can get yourself off easiest huh? She can't get the feelings she was feeling from herself very easily. And that pisses her off in the end and then she feels like there is something wrong with her like she weak or flawed. There may even be times when she craves that connection with someone so bad that she'll let her guard down around shitty guys who will treat her like shit but because they tell her how nice she and that she is pretty a few times she'll convince herself that's what she wants. For a while.

    So, just don't hurt her.

    In short…Chill the fuck out. Slow the fuck down. Think things out, preferably at times when you don't have your compass pointing north. Think about the other person for a change.

And I know you won't write back to this.
And that's okay.

Just know I love you, and I'm happy to be here for you anytime you need the kick in the ass. Like right now. Because you sure don't get it from just a tickling of the ass now did you. :)

Love,
Trace

>>>>
>
>
>
>

Subj:	**a little help...**
Date:	Sat. 6/05/2004 4:23:57 PM EST
From:	ssspellman@everydaysanctuary.net
To:	theigal@everydaysanctuary.net

Dude, Trace, help me out...
So I was with this girl...and as we were getting into it she just kept playing around near my butt...and I don't know why. I mean I was up her shirt and down her pants doing the deed and she can't do the same? Why can't I find a normal girl?
Anyway, we were getting all hot and I was doing my job on her, but she didn't give the same...and I don't know what to think. Was she just trying to get some from me? Why would she think I like butt stuff? I can't talk to any of the guys about this without getting shit. But seriously, what is wrong with her...or me??

sim

Subj: Taz IM
Date: Sun. 6/13/2004 9:58:48 PM EST
From: ssspellman@everydaysanctuary.net
To: ssspellman@everydaysanctuary.net

DevilLAX35: y the hell u go and ditch out last nite
DevilLAX35: and what the hell were u doin out wit that asschick last nite
castaspell: whats it matter becky asked if I wanted 2g2c spiderman2
DevilLAX35: did she grab ur ass since thats what ur down wit now
castaspell: haha
castaspell: no its all good
DevilLAX35: u should go to a scary movie so u could sit on her lap when u get scared make it easier
castaspell: fuck off Taz, shes cool
DevilLAX35: whateva
DevilLAX35: just make sure u bring protection for her strap on
castaspell: what the fucks your problem thomas?
DevilLAX35: no whats ur problem pusspellman
DevilLAX35: hanging around with that fag and asspeter
DevilLAX35: whats next dykemusic
castaspell: what are you talking about
DevilLAX35: is assbecky ur compromise, girlboy
DevilLAX35: i kno you been around that towelfag lately
castaspell: how'd you know that?
DevilLAX35: dont matter
DevilLAX35: sanchez just told me he saw you
castaspell: when? ok so?
DevilLAX35: he was like i saw spelly having dinner with a fruit like it was a fucking date
DevilLAX35: so what thefuck is up with you
castaspell: nothing
DevilLAX35: what the fucks happened to you
castaspell: whats it to you? nothings fucking happened. Just friends with ashad.
DevilLAX35: so thats its fucking name
castaspell: shut up!

DevilLAX35: just saying you better not turn fruit is all, and you better not be pullin this shit come seasonitme
DevilLAX35: and
DevilLAX35: dont be showing your face round the park or parties anytime soon if u know whats good for u
castaspell: what do you mean? what this before next season bullshit?
DevilLAX35: well come if u want 2 but ull get wicked thrashed if dont watch it
castaspell: goddamit
castaspell: you fucking suck
DevilLAX35: fuck you pussy
DevilLAX35: you seem like the one sucking it
castaspell: FUCK YOU ASSHOLE
DevilLAX35: fuck off fag
DevilLAX35: go cry 2 ur boyfriend

Subj:	**Re: wicked nasty**
Date:	Sun. 6/13/2004 11:06:20 PM EST
From:	Travis.Coleman@everydaysanctuary.net
To:	"Simon" ssspellman@everydaysanctuary.net

Condoms? Weird, although I guess I could see that. Bet the tip could work for a good Fipple
Yea that is freaky though about the breakage thou. Could be like cheating in class thou. don't be stupid and you wont get caught right so, basically don't go for fucking DDs and shit with your waterboobs

So yea, Fridays going to kick some serious fucking ASS! Yea, 18 on the 18th!!
Bring Becky if you wanna or else find someone else there that will want to moan around you…and not just cause she has to deal with being around you. jk

peace out boy scout
ttyl bro

>>>>
>
>
>
>

Subj:	**Re: wicked nasty**
Date:	Sun. 6/13/2004 4:54:13 PM EST
From:	ssspellman@everydaysanctuary.net
To:	Travis.Coleman@everydaysanctuary.net

Ah that does suck for that dude on the T. they don't have to be pervs to do that might be a dare or a prankparty or someshit...fuck, good thing it didn't pop on a latenight drunkfucker train thou. Actually, and don't tell Taz and them this and shit but I actually met a couple guys hangin in harv sq once that did that shit for a college prank party or whateva and they used condoms and had the same beef. they were all pretty coo actually Makes you wonder hwo safe thefcukrs are ifthey cant hold a b cup of h2o, you know?

Anyway cool thou youz had agoodtime, good thing thou you got the fcuk out of dodge thou , i hear quinz cops suck. and yea that was this chick becky, pretty cool girl, don't know whats up with her, just seeing how goes so yea walked hre home and hit up bball party, and yea no on enjoying that chicks moanings and shit, she was nasty, way way nasty.

Peace out cub scout

sime

Subj:	**wicked nasty**
Date:	Sun. 6/13/2004 12:09:45 PM EST
From:	Travis.Coleman@everydaysanctuary.net
To:	"Simon" ssspellman@everydaysanctuary.net


```
Fuck that is nasty!  So you had to just stay
there and listen to it?  Goddamn son, so,n
vicariously you got to experience some action
last night.  Damn man, you and your fucking
stories.  Even when they don't involve you
lol so what you went over there after the
movie with...oh, btw, who was the cute girly
you were with on moody, we saw you   didn't
you get loud and nasty wit her? Too bad if
not, she looked hot
```

So it was fucking stupid last night, get this, so we're on the Red Line going coming back from the party and we're all approaching the Park St station and there are these fuckin kids, all acting stupid and this chick, or what we thought was a chick, who is all like superstacked and is all skanking on her friends and being all supergirly and then bam, I kid you not, her tit starts leaking and shrinking. The whole car goes silent, they were all sitting rightnext to the door so a ton of people could see, and then bam, this little kid down the row breaks the silence and is like to his mom, "mommy…that girl isn't a girl" It was so fucking funny.. Wouldn't want to be him thou. They all rushed off and got off at the stop, probably on the way to a CVS for a refill or something, a balloon or two or whatever it is they use. the guys couldn't shutup about it, laughing and going off about the pervs and shit all the way back home. But yea Sanchezs bro Brians party was tight for a while, you remember him right. the house scored a keg and we all got hammered but ended up leaving after some crashers all stared brawling and shit with the north quincy fuckres that came too good thing to cause we caught the last train back to the rail back not wanting to do another one of those Taz drunkdriving adventures. so yea, pretty stupid night all in all, howd you go with the chick? get any or were you just collect some goss and not making some?

Trav

Subj:	**Re: btw**
Date:	Sun. 6/13/2004 11:08:12 PM EST
From:	Travis.Coleman@everydaysanctuary.net
To:	"Simon" ssspellman@everydaysanctuary.net

```
yea, stay the fuck away from my sisters.
dickmunch.
and no, definately not family, so sonds like i
could do her to huh.  Game On!  I could go up
to her like, I have so much to learn, tutor
me, hey and if you marry me you don't have to
change your name.  huh def a good selling
point
So dude, whats her goods be like?  1QQk at you
with girls all ova the fucking state

t



>>>>
>
>
>
>
```

Subj:	**btw**
Date:	Sun. 6/13/2004 4:55:49 PM EST
From:	ssspellman@everydaysanctuary.net
To:	Travis.Coleman@everydaysanctuary.net

oh hey real quick, you know anyone in your fam named danielle coleman?
met this in amherst this wkend who this friendof mine from this sociology of sex class or something they had together. Shes fucking HOT and took a sex class! ;) anyway I just scored her email addy, thought maybe there might be the inside rote thru you, or any warnings or fuckoffs

know she can't be a sis so then alls fair game right? heehee :)
let me know
oh and I don't know about friday yet, I'll try to get off work for it, time to start the 18th bdays baby!!

peace out
sim

Subj:	**Ashad superfucking IM**
Date:	Thr. 6/17/2004 2:49:24 AM EST
From:	ssspellman@everydaysanctuary.net
To:	ssspellman@everydaysanctuary.net

…accid cut closed start of convo

    castaspell: I dunno
    ashad04: Seriously though Simon, whats the point of a bunch of people thinking they have better security if you all are as dumb as a box of rocks and not even worth the effort to 'terrorize?'
    castaspell: ?
    ashad04: All the money spent on stupid shit while school budgets are cut, just as an example. So like I say, fucking poor stupid bastards are the only ones that think they need protection and "security" from the world, because they're the only ones that have no fucking clue whats going on and keep messing things up and pissing everyone off, but they are also the ones that generally aren't a strategic target for anyone sane and violent. They'll still get someone coming after them, but those are opportunists, not 'terrorists trying to destroy the way of life' of America. By being ignorant passive and perpetually favoring the wrong side, there is nothing of a way of life to destroy when you go around pissing in your own pool as much as you are.
    castaspell: hey ashad, all apolgies and shit, but I have no idea what ever you are fuckigntalking about
    ashad04: Well the same thing happened during the last Bush, and with Reagan, and with any president who plays with real GIs like they are GI Joes. Cyncially I can say that the weather and which groups of people are considered good or bad are about the only things that have changed in the States in the past fifty years…there are lots of fun things to occupy your attention and a lot of information at hand to learn from, but are most people better off now than a generation ago…no. At best, the people like

your parents are about static with where they were then I would wager.

    castaspell: yea I guess so but so what isnt' that everywhere?

    ashad04: Simply its this, everyone is focused on "protecting America's interests," but rarely does anyone stop to think if America's interests should be examined and changed.

    ashad04: Only an idiot keeps playing their golf game la-de-da like nothings wrong when there as thunderstorms come up and everyone else takes the hint.

    castaspell: Wel I know that this country has a lot messed up with it, but I mean I think we all work for the same stuff and want the same things right? Mistakes always happen but its for the common good of freedom and all that right?.

    ashad04: Where'd you pull that egoboosting pretentious quote from? It doesn't sound like you. There weren't enough "fucks" and way too many lame, old, overused cliches in it to be you. You go for the fresh 99 cent kiosk references

    ashad04: and I see you think you are able to accurately speak for everyone in within the country.

    ashad04: That's usually the first warning sign of someone about to do some really stupid shit.

    castaspell: I know there are differences and stuff but how could it be much better with all the shit going on?

    ashad04: Are you joking?

    ashad04: Let me ask you this, how many friends do you have that are Arab, Asian, or Indian, besides me?

    castaspell: why does it matter? a few

    ashad04: It matters for one because half of Moody Street is Middle Eastern or Asian... and I would wager you couldn't even place them on a map confidently let alone say that you have learned much about them individually that is distinct from anyone you regularly were around.

    castaspell: hey thats not fair thou

    ashad04: and two, because you use words that are thrown around so often without explanation that they lose all good description, and you're right, no its not fair, but its realistic nonetheless, "Freedom" "Security" what do they mean to you? I bet your version of how to achieve them and what they are are entirely different than someone who has been followed and has to have their parents tell you not to make any sudden movements or do anything suspicious in government buildings (including your own schools) because you might get picked up as a "material wintness" for questioning .

    castaspell: well if you know all of that, how do you get everyone to have the same idea of freedom and security then?

    ashad04: That's easy. It's called "communication"

    ashad04: Look, I know its hard, I've done it with several different cultures, but it's the same the world over, you simply have to actively want to know people. Look you don't even need "security" if you actually understand everyone around you and there is respect.

    castaspell: well I know that

    ashad04: You say you do but do you really? You live in a country with a leader that is actively going for keeping the fight on and to keep it on in other people's backyards to protect your own plants.

    ashad04: And the worst comes when you realize everyone else can see through your façade, that's when people get unpredictable. Like you lately.

    castaspell: what?

    ashad04: You're scared to have people know you, so to protect yourself you often push away any threat to really get into the good stuff with them, and it seems like there are a few things we could talk about that might help that but first you have got to promise me something…

    castaspell: um, yes?

    ashad04: Don't throw any hissyfits with anything I say okay?

    ashad04: Basically, I'm about to go off on some things and you just gotta chill out on typing out some kneejerk responses or getting pissed an signing off…I won't be mean, okay? Just throwing out ideas and perceptions, cool?

    castaspell: okay mighty midnight professor

    ashad04: ha, anyway

ashad04: With a thousand different languages comes a thousand different ways to communicate love, hate, fear, hope, but in the end they are all saying the same things. You know this inherently with your latent Jewish background. You've grown up with several identities incorporated into a whole. But its not as conscious for you because of the your ability to squeeze by without any particular being too vidid...but still you occasionally struggle when any one tries to assert superiority over another...

ashad04: ...which is why you were attracted to George W initially, because he was offering a way for so many parts of you that are often tugged back and forth to feel on common ground (as long as they were willing to disregard the parts of you that identity with whatever population is distasteful)...

ashad04: The problem is that it's a negative identity and to give you a image, as fake as the old west town in old western movies. He banks his votes on people who partly by accident but more and more by choice, do not identify themselves with gays or arabs as examples. It requires you to unidentify with other groups of people to be excited about someone promising security. There is only one way you get security since it is an illusion, you stage a drama and you find yourself an antagonist.

ashad04: And hold your horses, I'm not done...

castaspell: k

ashad04: No different than if we were in Germany a hundred years ago and some Catholic bishop was trying to get us to feel a part of a Greater Germany in a pogrom against the enemies of a prosperous Christian community. And I think you know where I'm going with that one.

castaspell: yes I do. Got it. ok go on... you are going to tie it up yes?

ashad04: Ah, but of course. I see I have your attention now... Okay...

castaspell: oh you always have my attention

ashad04: okay, that's what I like to hear...

castaspell: thought so

ashad04: It comes down to this, you have to be able to look at everyting from different perspectives. Objective isn't otally possible or appealing, but just picture taking a step back, and if your efforts and desires can't stand up against that sort of test without looking as bad as the things that you call wrong then they are not any better...

ashad04: Its like this...notice how easy it is throwing the generic descriptions around for everything that people do to you to indict them for hurting people. But then in calling your equal actions against them something else and you're allowing the same thing to be acceptable just by using a familiar cliche, a rug and a nice fragrance to be thrown over your pile of shit so you think it's a better pile or maybe not even a pile of shit at all...

ashad04: Following me so far?

castaspell: at a distance...

castaspell: oh wait...I mean, oh yes of course, professor...please continue

ashad04: :) Good, okay then. Here is where it can be shown in specific...

ashad04: Good and beautiful parts abound in Massachusetts and Boston, but the most condemnable elements are the ghettoing people do in their minds and the loneiness and unsurity in their hearts they attempt to fill in bad ways. The same story simply in a different costume, but worse here than most others.

ashad04: People like how Taz's family seem to be get the way they do because they choose to make their concept of community so narrow and strict, and because they do not understand what is outside that narrow scope they are anxious, concerned and worried about it, the natural human tendency with things we don't understand, and then lumping them together. Like you with gays, hippies and vegetarians...

castaspell: shocking. shocking you would bring that soy tidbit into it.

ashad04: I know, but it's such a fun phobia to make fun of :) But the central point is this: With that narrow identity and fear of the misunderstood they cannot grow up and that is really the only 'escape' They only focus on false and superficial attempts to escape and separate themselves from all those they say they are so different and better than. Whether it be Muslims or gays today or

Catholics or Chinamen a hundred years ago they end up creating artificial barriers against the things that they fear or feel uneasy about which can never truly stand up against the test of time...

    ashad04: But it is not the other group that they truly fear, it is inside themselves, because how to you secure yourself away from an idea, or ideal? You can't. But you sure can put the blame on someone.. That is why whenever that fear is stirred up and aggression comes out it gets so far out of control and the group gets tighter and smaller...

    ashad04: WWII for the United States was overall a war against the Nazis and Japan Why the distinction between Nazi and the average German by not between Imperial warmachine Japanese and the common Japanese person? There isn't even a commonly known term to describe the fucked-up Japanese players of WWII. You could claim Imperialists, but still, its not a distinguished group. A bit fishy, no?

    castaspell: Hmm...I see what you mean, never thought about it in that way

    ashad04: Once fear is stoked nothing done as a direct action of it can extinguish it...that's how the US was able ot pretty much fuck with everybody in Asia directly except for the Chinese. Pesky buggers had to go get organized quick. But yea, all those groups of people scapecoated are just excuses. They are like NiQuil. It doesn't do anything to cure what is going on inside as much as it numbs you up so you are knocked out which may help you get through it. But when you start relying on it as a cure, you end up waking up late for work from having too much, with a hangover, a hell of an OTC tab and most likely an infection that is worse due to what you've just done to yourself.

    ashad04: Sound a bit familiar doesn't it when you start replacing those terms with Iraq, waking up in 2004 with a hangover wondering why worldwide let alone domestically we're all worse off than 2001, and 100s billion dollars later...

    castaspell: wow, yea that is messed up I guess...

    ashad04: And here is an interesting anecdote. You know how the medivel Spaniards decided their problems were all because of the Jews? Did you know that the Grand Inquisitor ended up becoming Pope?

    castaspell: No...really? That's fucked up.

    ashad04: Yea it definitely is, I have a book full of that sort of stuff if you want to borrow it just let me know.

    ashad04: And so I'll tie that in simply saying that that kind of Pope seems on the surface of titles and institituion to be a eminent source of wisdom etc, but would be the worst possible person to follow in formulating a personal concept of humanity and who and what that may include. Likewise, Ashcrofts and Cheneys and Rumsfelds having been involved in what they have in the past are less trustworthy to anyone that doesn't subscibe to their narrow notions of puesdo-religious myths like Manifest Destiny and new ones made up like the Bush Doctrine with his whole "Crusade" shit. Further profits in the end are their real messiah.

    ashad04: ok, that was a bit rambly...

    castaspell: really? hadn't noticed. was about to tell you to slow the fuck down :)

    ashad04: Oh hush you

    ashad04: But in a world changing as quickly as this one, those that have a strict and an unwillingness to alter perception of the way things ought to be are the worst to have at the helm. You don't take big rigid ships into choopier waters that become curvy and rapid like.

    castaspell: hey, good one :)

    ashad04: Hey I like this too tired to type Simon...means you aren't getting in the way of open eyes. So I'll continue...

    castaspell: please do, just chillin here munching

    ashad04: Any person is in a position of power like that can find themselves abusing it so easy if they're not careful. But with that potential for abuse, the danger comes when people are so confident in themselves and their actions that they feel they can do no wrong, because, and here we go, it's a fight between "good and evil" and a wonder isn't it that everyone thinks they are all on the same side of "good?" Then why is it they inevitably end up fighting each other over it?

ashad04: If all religions claim to be right and all are human inventions, then how can any one of them be above the hubris of pride and error that leads to identifying the self against the "other" with that eternal danger of manifested pride coming around…unfortunately now with automatic firearms and nuclear weapons instead of sticks and rocks.

castaspell: yea rocks and stricks are so underrated. And you nned to quit this college thesis bigword thing…or I'll Go BaCk To SoMe of my tricks

ashad04: haha okay, but seriously…

ashad04: And what I am about to say is not an attack or an insult, but merely the observations of you. Okay?

castaspell: ok. So warned :)

ashad04: Your problem in particular is connected to all of this Simon. That is, you seem to go along with whatever the barometer says for the most part. Which is good. Because you are involved in several camps and definitely feel whats going on. But it's when any of those camps requires those allied to it to express that fear, you find yourself vulnerable to do so…

castaspell: well that is obvious, that's everyone right?

ashad04: Oh yes, definitely. Its Kerry's doubleedged sword. But see, the difference is he doesn't go around waving it around thinking he is the shit. He knows a lot of shit and probably has a good ego, but he doesn't rely on such a narrow filter of perspectives.

ashad04: 'It take a village' for a reason. None of us are that "badass" by ourselves as you would say.

castaspell: yea i dont know about Kerry still.

ashad04: And that's fine.

ashad04: That's the way it should be, because you are just recently learning more about him. But at least he's been doing lots of shit successfully for 30 years. That's why this isn't a full election as much as it is a Vote of No Confidence for Bush. So, wait until the head to head comes out and see who has less principles. For me, I'm just waiting for the Bush people to start trying to go after Kerry like they did McCain and you'll see true colors flying high and see people sick of it.

castaspell: yea I guess so

ashad04: as brutishly realistic as I am at times, I am confident that the country can't tolerate Bushes for too long.

ashad04: I once heard Bill Maher say of Bush that he seemed like the boss's son, the guy that gets a corner office and just comes in one day and fires you because he can.

ashad04: well cutely dumb and naïve as you are little Simon, you actually have the chance to help *fire* him this year. What a birthday present to yourself.

castaspell: yea that is kinda cool. Thats funny to think about.

ashad04: So yea, I know this flaw of character rather well…

ashad04: Because I've had very similar experiences, but as a consequence of having more extreme opposing outward "identities" that were encouraged but were more vivid and apparent I was not able to mask them and migrate from one to another as smoothly or coyly as you or to occupy several at once which seems to be your forte, both gift and curse.

ashad04: okay, your turn to talk

ashad04: wait, sorry, gotta play the part.

ashad04: Okay, are there any question so far, students?

castaspell: yea yea, um no. but…

castaspell: yea Iguess I forget about that a lot, get absorbed into whatever and lose track of time. I've wondered about you though, no offense, but I've always been afraid to ask you what your family is like with you being gay and all.

ashad04: None taken…another story for another night…but suffice to say that that was a cake walk compared to the subculture here or there that is strictly trying to remain their concept of identity. But they go to far with it in the end and are more extreme than is healthy.

ashad04: perhaps like overly overt and obvious New York Jews or the 80s Boston Irish Catholic contingent?

castaspell: yea, go with the hyper-term for the crazy ones there, don't know much bout the whole Boston thing thou. You really play with your words a bit much don't you?

ashad04: but I do it well. That's why its okay.

ashad04: But one mention with the "crazy ones"

ashad04: It isn't any one of people's fault, to be born and raised that way...only when they start actively going with it. All they have to do is move past it. But the problem is its hard, of course, with hundreds of years of European habit imbedded in them (not having the slightest clue what was happening in the world outside of their borders til it was up on their pretty Spanish or Austrian doorsteps.)

ashad04: Sound a bit familiar with the overly obscene "knockknock who's there" a few years ago, yes?

castaspell: yea true, good comp

ashad04: But back on the couch with you Mr. Spellman, my important impatient patient ...

castaspell: So now we're out of the classroom? Ok...just don't make me quack like a duck or anything.

ashad04: hmmm...mental note: quack like a duck. (tucked away for later consideration) Okay..going forward...

castaspell: haha

ashad04: So I suppose, think of anything specifically that goes on in Mass right now. While most people are going in blindly, assimilating themselves and accepting the malfunctioning status quo without question, it is because they only conceive of a very limited cultural inclusion that they are a part. (That is also the reason why it is so quickly overvalued or overemphasised as well, where ideas and ideals quickly turn into out of control ideology and idol worship)...

castaspell: ToO CoLlEgEiSh...

ashad04: Okay Okay...asshole

ashad04: Its this...

ashad04: You are actively trying to fit in somewhere...wherever feels "right" which is to say where it is comfortable and encouraged and approvable. And that is what messes you up so bad. Problem is, any legitimate "camp" will advertise themselves as "right." (That is the sign that they are just as clueless as you)

castaspell: yea thats what it feels like def

ashad04: what it with those defs...Okay, its like this...

ashad04: I had a great time with you May17th. We all did. But you have to ask yourself, why. I figured out the next time I saw you…what would have happened if instead of us dropping by that day and inviting you to come with, Taz came by and invited you to a spiritual service organized to "protect the sanctity of marriage" You would have been very tempted to go, and would have felt the encouragement to consider yourself a part of the group, because people you care about are in it, and their talking about security and protecting good things like marriage and the right way to live and that its jus tthis easy, just be against this thing (removing all consideration of empathy of people affected because if they are against us they are not for protecting good things that are the foundation of civilized society, and with work we'll be able to convince you they are sub-human…depending on how far we end up going with this).

castaspell: yea your probably rigth

ashad04: It comes down to this. Be nervous any time anyone loves humanity but can't stand human beings. And…

ashad04: Be careful anytime anyone professes the immediate need to put an ideology or principle above anything that has feelings. It all comes back to City Slickers concept.

castaspell: you lost me

ashad04: look you can't always just lose yourself in the details, you lose yourself that way, but not in the good transcendental way. I bet you're the type that when have to go to a Catholic funeral or wedding will do the charade on yourself like everyone else am I right?

castaspell: well yea sometimes…so? And I meant, where the hell are you going with city slickers?

ashad04: Soo…the believers do it on purpose as a symbol of something. You do it only to try and blend and not stick out. Oh…the City Slickers concept…

castaspell: ok

ashad04: You remember the scene when the drunk cowboys are going to shoot the calf in the head?

castaspell: yea okay vaguly

ashad04: The danger is in the willingness to find anything with feelings expendible because "its just a cow" or "just" a few terrorist suspects that are "enemy combatants" or "just" an acceptable level of unfortunate collateral damage that was once a small community of people in favor of a larger "objective of national interest" in someone else's nation...

ashad04: That cow could just as easily a few decades earlier been "just a couple of black girls" that were in the bombed church in your South, or the children of the "wild savages" who must taken and christianised and educated to "breed the black out of them" as was significantly still the case in 20th century America and Australia.

castaspell: dude where do you get all this shit?

ashad04: Me can read good, mista.

ashad04: books be good

ashad04: that be o.k. with you suh?

castaspell: lol, okay. Stop that

ashad04: I just take after you, my sassy sarcastic friend.

castaspell: I like your City Slicker ref though, never thought of it like that.

ashad04: So yea back to you...you are simply a unknown quantity, a free agent of sorts. Every group which you are involved with even minimally encourages you to join them, but at the same time will look at you funny when you start exhibiting thigns they don't understand from parts of themselves that you respresent that they attach to the other groups that make them uneasy.

castaspell: Hmm...yea your right I guess, sucks but what can you do

ashad04: And that is okay. It is okay to be like that. It's like this though:

ashad04: Why I have trouble getting upset around people like Taz anymore, because I understand that fear and that confusion he has inside, I've felt it for just about everyone at one point or another :) So I understand it in him, and I understand it in you too.

ashad04: and if I did get angry and write someone like that off for voicing what he believes at that time I'm closing all chances of connecting to the person. Make sense?

ashad04: Not to harp on my experiences, but I grew up with a blood fued between myself and every American in my head. But I matured and didn't only rely on the information from that same category. Evnetually I was able to grow a spinal cord emotionally and intellectually.

castaspell: really? You were anti-American? Did you ever burn any flags?

ashad04: Yes. Oh no no, this was all when I was still very much knee-high. Understand, just as you were too young to remember the Gulf War but you have the a grasp of the feelings and whatnot and have always had Saddam as a bad guy, I never knew of any other way than being against the United States and questionable against most of the Western world. Saddam has been your boogieman since you started watching the news, so you were much like me, except I had a couple hundred million boogiemen with missles and bad attitudes to focus on...

castaspell: So after we left Tehran, my parents enrolled me in a good school outside of London that made me meet kids of al sorts. All of a sudden I had friends that I'd been told were my enemy.

ashad04: I didn't meet David the Jew or Denise daughter of an Anglican lord, but I was meeting David, my friend who taught me to swim or Denise who wanted me to be one of her afternoon tea-time friends.

ashad04: Without knowing it, I had learned that you have to rationalise yourself to yourself. And that you can be a bit sporty and a bit posh at the same time. :)

ashad04: I must say, it's a lot easier when you're not surrounded by insulated fear and hate. (Like here with 9/11 bullshit) You just can't get as headstrong when the most aggressive and emotive language all of a sudden becomes wankers and stumpets and the like and isn't directed at a group as much as it just rotates to who just tripped or spilled something :) But so when it seems I am harping and critical on you, it is simply trying to explain it out in ways to make sense. (For instance as you try to do a balancing act, since I grew up with anti-American, it was something I could have in common with the British, so I got some comfort and belonging at the expense of singling out that group. That's what got me into David Bowie initially :)

castaspell: yea ok, gotcha... I can imagine you being all cool bashing us round helping those brit boys like you ;)

ashad04: Yea but a tough act to keep up however. But so keep that in mind as you flip through the channels...you have that satellite service with at least the BBC I would imagine, so you can get your head poked outside the insulation from time to time, and should do so.

castaspell: yea I definitely want to, just always forget when I plop on the couch after work

ashad04: Late nights? I could see you getting into "Coupling" so check that show out some late night. (trust me) ;)

castaspell: I know the feeling of switching homes when young, not that sort of extreme I guess but yea guess its never a cake walk or anything

ashad04: It's a tough balancing act, yes. But whenver you get frustrated or don't think you can do it. Look at it this way: You learned to walk didn't you? You learned to ride a bicycle and a skateboard didn't you? Tough balancing acts that you can learn.

castaspell: yea I guess that's tru

ashad04: Although some chimps can do it too, so don't think you're too cool

castaspell: Oh shut up...

ashad04: and can probably type better than you as a matter of fact

castaspell: you can never drop the typing shit can you
castaspell: brb

ashad04: Well I'm not a tight ass with everything, so relax, but if you just quit being so lazy on the keyboard when your talking to me it woudn't be a problem, just trying to help you practice looking sma-hhat, you can still get your LaMe TyPiNg KiCks elsewhere if you want to. I'm not training you for my health.

asahd04: And fuck Simon, that is fucking annoying trying to type like that. Do you actually spend that much time and care being barely readable and unarticulate? Just as easily you could breeze through normal lingo and be bettering your brilliance?

castaspell: ok back...and no I don't actually type LiKe that...fucking annoys me...but you talking about unreadable writing in this fucking font of yours...

castaspell: and so now you're training me now huh? And why is that?

ashad04: This font is a bit difficult I give you. However, I can't remember how to change it (everytime I try it reverts back automatically to the save preferences or something like that) and my computer-savy friend Steve is out of town until the fall semester starts. Face it, I'm a panzy when it comes to the tech.

ashad04: And the reason why? For your health of course.

ashad04: and for my amusement

ashad04: You're like my Koko

ashad04: :-P

castaspell: who the fuck is Koko?

ashad04: Koko is a gorilla that can sign language, she doesn't have a full understanding of proper English sentence construction or verb rules, ahh...wait, sounds like someone I know. But I bet she could critique your typed-out "English" too. :)

castaspell: Dude, that's fucing weak busting out with a monkey insult

ashad04: well I didn't actually. Gorillas are apes, not monkeys. So it wasn't that weak considering you're just pissed because you can't win and you couldn't even have a come back without an error or two.

castaspell: God, no shit. Yea okay enough!

ashad04: :)

castaspell: oh my Alah, Ashad whent for a smiley face out of textcontext...what is the world coming to? Not English-snob Ashad! That's a Wicked Pissa!!!

ashad04: First off: Good come back...However...

castaspell: you must have had drill sargents as teachers in school.

ashad04: That's Allah; and no you better not ever try to acronym him into that bullshit cyber language you would think passes for its own linguistic category; and that I bet you misspelled just to take the piss; that was without reference back to a subject, not "textcontext"; also that was a poor preposition end of sentence (which is okay at times - like Ands, Buts, Wells, Sos, and You're such a wanker when you... - but not to the degrees and ways you use them); and lastly, that is sergeant, you phonetically-dependent sad statement of the substandard schooling being done in this country. And if I had, I would tell you to do 20 pushups or type "I'm Ashad's lazy and linguistically-challenged charity case friend" 50 times and there will be no using CTL-A, C, and V, mister!

    castaspell: Oooo...that took a while...I thought I actually had hit a nerve! Damnnn...was all about to ask which nerve is that? Where is the button located exactly so I can toy with it anytime you need to :)

    ashad04: You're fun because you can take out the piss and take in some at the same time. You're a good bloke like that, Simon Spellman.

    ashad04: What's your middle name by the way?
    castaspell: Stanley
    ashad04: Oh, so that three "s" addresss has a reason. Nice.
    castaspell: Yea
    ashad04: And I wouldn't let you know you hit a nerve anway, but I'm not too worried about that for you have not the talent or the expertise yet in your young years to pose that threat or risk.

    castaspell: oh whatever
    ashad04: Also the reason I would have never have followed through on all the flirtations as you are too innocent and delicate for the time being...you'll discover the world on your own and in your own ways before you realise in your own time that that awesome arab Ashad was the dreamiest dude ever to enter my life.

    ashad04: Sometimes it's so nice knowing everything :)
    castaspell: linguistically-challenged Simon can only muster: Rrrriiiiiight...

    ashad04: Ahh...I'm flattered. You actually took the time to scroll up and correctly use that jab back at me. The most sincere flattery yet. When you start typing just like me I'll know my time and attention was well spent ;)

    castaspell: ahh...perfect. Mental note: Mimic Ashad for bankable tease points.

ashad04: Hah!! You only used bankable because you couldn't spell "guarantee" with confidence huh??
castaspell: asshole
ashad04: thought so
castaspell: O:-)
ashad04: Yes you better be putting your little angelic symbol of who is in charge of this conversation up there.
castaspell: :-P
ashad04: But actually as you brought it up I'll give you this, I had a rough time of it as puberty hit and a few school changes made me a blatant "other" to just about every person.
castaspell: really? Do tell...
ashad04: Okay...well besides being the new kid, I could end up being the brownnose darky or even just the teachers' pet kind of kid since I always had to ask questions to clarify the fucking poshy language they were confined to, or the last picked for whatever it was no-talent sort of kid, the jihad kid, the poffy kid, etc. And it got better as everyone learned new ones. Eventually I could become the son of the son of a bitch who killed another kids daddy or daddy's daddy in wars of independence in this country or that. (those were the most entertaining, because the kids never could even pronounce the place which they were referring)
castaspell: dude sounds like it could be rough then
ashad04: I learned the hard way that you have to find comfort in discomfort and form an inclusive zone that will never be totally secure. I noticed a lot of people in the desperate need for that belonging would join up with one social clique category or another and for all I know could easily have turned out as 'urban hicks' as you so accurately and matter-of-factly have put it. (even if poshly urban hicked)
ashad04: I hope you will be able to keep from falling off into any one direction like that. You are very special. But you are also very vulnerable.
castaspell: damn, mate. I stayed home for a peaceful quiet night after a hectic week...shouldn't have gotten online :)
castaspell: enjoying listening to you thou. You can get all deep and shit.

ashad04: deep and shit? Who else are you talking to now?

castaspell: what do you mean? I mean you say stuff that makes me think

ashad04: and I mean who else are you chatting with online? All of a sudden you talkin wit a diffrnt flava, G

castaspell: noone got online, got a phonecall for a mom thou

ashad04: That's what I'm talking about!!

castaspell: what? Dude chill out and shit…

ashad04: Sorry Sim, and I'm not upset, just trying to highlight and pinpoint a little something…

ashad04: Don't stress and bottle up, it's okay to certain degrees, just take care to watch that you don't go overboard without a rope, you dope.

castaspell: Alright. Sorry mate. My bad. I will try to watch it with you.

ashad04: That's all actually what I was getting at, happy u can go n b all Simon G for a min…

ashad04: It's about the fact that too often you're like a fucking chameleon, and just make sure you got a part of you that is a good baseline. You're like a superhero version of a follower. You don't just follow. You charge right in, wherever there is anything to be followed, you'll be there! And that's fine for a while, a lot of good people start out that way. And I know, because I've been there. We all have been there (the problem is a lot of people are still there), so be warned…the problem comes when you are still there when your not paying attention for a year, a few years, a lifetime and you haven't learned to figure out directions and how to open doors on your own

castaspell: LoL…I'm the lizard super hero…I go commando style to protect all the girls in the shower, all over the world!

ashad04: there ya go, way to use your powers for good!

ashad04: But seriously, just realize how much your typing goes to shit and looks lazy and slangy when you get excited or agitated, tired or depressed, so you're not actually thinking as much about what your saying and have it be accurate to what your thoughts or feeling inside are…

ashad04: The more you do that the less people will really understand what you think or feel and you will start feeling anxious about it and slowly walls go up because you are scared of being more misunderstood…

castaspell: shit, dogg…slow down

ashad04: you are more just broadcasting your immediate thought and knee-jerk impressions. It's cool in degrees and in moderation. We all need to just say things are fucking cool or fucking weak sometimes and leave it at that and go off about something else…But you change with the wind direction and temperature.

castaspell: whatever you say

ashad04: Just hear me out and then I promise to shut up?

ashad04: You have to learn the real shit with the altered shit before its good shit or deep shit. Did I say it in the way you understand it now?

castaspell: yea yea playa I hear yaz :)

ashad04: :) I'm saying it all lighthearted too, but I was only slightly joking when I said that training bit earlier. And before I go off you have to promise not to even start typing a response until I've actually sent you what I'm writing and you've read the whole thing and taken at least one breath of ponder time before you begin your finger-tapping and backspacing, okay?

castaspell: Ok Ok. I promise. I'll sit on my hands. Oooo.

ashad04: Ok…yes, you do that.

ashad04: Just keep this all in mind: Communication is key. Being in the drivers seat, *and* being able to be a good driver allows you to belong wherever you wish, allows you to adapt out of choice, not out of a need to not stick out. The most beautiful thing you can be is a quite ordinary looking and yet extraordinary. That on the general life theme, but specifically too I will say this.

ashad04: You will never be able to hold good relationships with anyone special or feel comfortable and stable with a lot of people or a group that are deep-hearted and critical-thinkers that can know you on many levels if you don't have a good foundation, and that you are aware of as being rock hard, *and* then on top of it, that you then actually know a lot of cool shit which you know is the thing that really tweaks your melon.

    ashad04: Like a cherry on top :)

    castaspell: What do you mean?

    castaspell: what do you mean by find rockhard you, like what…where?

    ashad04: You need to figure out what is important to you, and you need to make that unnegoiatable, make it stick. Don't be a male version of the girls that just straight project an image out and allow it to be altered depending on the person desired and for the affirmation needed. It's the car/driver thing again. You are already living, already showing yourself, just make sure you know what your showing. You flickfreak, understand this. You need to be every level you can be of the production of your show.

    castaspell: Yea, but how do you do that without looking like a rigid little tightass though?

    ashad04: Well of course it you can't only do that…you also are the principle player of the show and play different parts here and there depending on circumstances…

    ashad04: It's a balancing game, Simon. Think life should be simple?

    castaspell: well no, its not that but…just seems like you are just trying to make it harder.

    ashad04: Hmm. Well I think its like this…if you were forced to wear helmets playing soccer you would think it was making things harder right?

    castaspell: Yea of course,

    ashad04: Actually bad example, scratch that. Say you were in high school fifty years ago. You would have protested wearing so much gear. But as much as it makes things more difficult it opens up new possibilities. It's the same with the big general along with the small specific.

    castaspell: hmm, yea I suppose that's true, wouldn't be as aggressive or confident in fighting for the ball and stuff

    ashad04: Do you have a favorite movie? Do you have a favorite song? Yes…

    ashad04: Are they rock solid? No…

ashad04: They change with time, they change depending on mood or time of the day let alone who is around or what you are doing which is why the fucking terms like "favorite" anything get watered down so much and are so meaningless. You probably have ten favorite songs a few best friends and in the end there is no weight to it when try to put emphasis to the terms, but alas, I digress

castaspell: Yea I guess so … yea bad, Ashad, bad. No digressing for you!

ashad04: But…what is your favorite part of cuddling with someone and why? Who would you take with you for a weekend road trip in a car with a broken stereo or without mobile phone coverage?

ashad04: funny

ashad04: And I already know the answer to this one, so I will ask, What is it about Jenn or Angie or Tracy or me that you enjoy so much about when you talk with them that you couldn't get with other people?

castaspell: well I'd have to say that its the peaceful, quite arm-in-arm thing, being able to be close like that and not worry about all the crazy bullshit in life. And I guess I would say that it'd be fun to take a trip with

castaspell: damnnn…you're good.

ashad04: Yes, yes. I know. But don't worry, I, for one, use my powers for good.

ashad04: or for the naughty good sort of evil ;)

castaspell: I like how you go shameless and include yourself in there too

ashad04: Yea, me too :)

ashad04: But seriously, that's where it's at. There are some things which you will never be able to pinpoint for eternity, and the key is to stop trying, and stop beating yourself up over not being able and just accept it. But there are others that are deep, intrinsic elements of your being straight away When you resent someone, often is for the thing that they helped you bring out in yourself and you don't want to admit it to yourself. Intrapersonal scapecoating. Whenver you break up with someone it's because they are a "bitch" or whatnot, only later will you, while looking a little down, with hunched shoulders, start to admit you weren't exactly moviescene material, more like RealWorld material. And that's okay, that's part of you, and you just need to know it, thank Whomever you credit with creating you, so you don't lose it or abuse it or do bad things with it, and then stop apologizing for you being you

    ashad04: and work on making a newer, better version of you.
    castaspell: Yea I guess so. Never thought of it that way.
    ashad04: I rest my case. I'll shut up and let you absorb all that now from here to eternity.
    castaspell: how you get this insightful oh wise one.
    ashad04: Oh. That's simple Dogg...You Gots to know the Riiite peeps, then dogg, you can Kno yo heart, and Kno yo head. And kno da diffrence.
    castaspell: you're a dick sometimes you know that? :)
    ashad04: Of course I know it, 'cause I kno me heart and me head, young laddie :) okay...
    ashad04: It's like this Simon: Find out your strengths, be aware of your weaknesses, and go with that. What do those strapping little plastic men in uniform say, "knowing is half the battle?" Well get with it and get half your battle done with, soldier!
    ashad04: The sergeant has spoken!
    castaspell: fuck you are all over the place. what did I open up by using that damn word...
    ashad04: Oh you have no idea...but just go get your chevy chase in tha an get yo groove on. Isn't that the McBeal ONiel?
    castaspell: the what? oh I'm gonna call you on that shit! You aren't a fucking LockStock sortof bloke!! How is that any different than RBing and ghangsta.
    ashad04: There is no diff yo, but you gotta B downnn with the subtleties and the art of the shiznit! Anyone can drive a fucking turkey round town, or use a reference in a comment, but it's in the art of knowing how to do it and say something with it rather than just say it that matters. You are a fucking treasure chest of potential, but ya gotta get your groove on and pack the core to

the brim with some soulfood so you can be cruising tha mountan, rather than simply getting by on the sly with whats in the impulse isle.

    castaspell: damn boy! You were all ova da fuckin place with tha! Liking toppin it with the Pauly Shoreism I must say, bonus points for the balla.

    ashad04: For instance…as you just proved…

    ashad04: As much as you fight it or act like you're unaware of it, you are a story kid, and a snobby little story kid at that. but quoting a proper band's lyrcs, 'he's an addict and that's a fact, but at least he's not smoking crack'

    ashad04: To be crass, basically…

    ashad04: You get your rocks off with storytime.

    ashad04: and probably have been since Kindy-ga-den

    castaspell: THAT is definitely not something I'd ever picture you saying…what do you mean storytime, you read more than I do.

    ashad04: Yes I like stories too. But it doesn't do it for me like it does for you.

    ashad04: Look…

    ashad04: From what you've told me, history fascinates you. Chemistry doesn't. But learning about the discoveries or lives or the sordid gossip of chemists does. You hate French class, but you adored Amelie on so many levels beyond the adorable actress because of all the tiny stories (which really impressed me, and can work wonders with the girls too). Hint hint. Substance = snogging

    castaspell: thanks for the hint, cheers

    ashad04: And if ever it was obvious…you had yourself heaps of fun on the hll in front of Cambridge City Hall, but you wouldn't last five minutes inside of it for business as usual. But it was the whole mystique of what was going on in there in the bane, normal, business as usual issuing of marriage licenses that totally captivated you when that photographer came out with a camera full of adorable cake-cutting pictures. I saw that look on your face.

    ashad04: Face it:

    ashad04: you're a straight up, straight drama queen :)

castaspell: LOL yea I guess
ashad04: And a comedy junkie?
ashad04: And a television melodrama critic?
ashad04: And a lyric lover?
castaspell: ok i get the point
ashad04: and slowly becoming a literary coinsurer
ashad04: and a popculture addict and reference snob ;)
ashad04: better watch it on that last one...your abbreviationistic and surfacelevel rants smell the same as the rest
castaspell: everyone is as holy as thee and thou
ashad04: Hey, well said.
castaspell: Ashad...
ashad04: Yes?
castaspell: UR like SO Wick-ed smaaa-t
ashad04: Hush you
castaspell: UR LiKe SOO My HeRo aNd StUfF
ashad04: Cut that shit out you wick-ed Wank-a Bass-tad
castaspell: too-shay, moan-a-me
ashad04: You're a little tarty for a sheltered saltine treasure of a drama queen aren't you?
castaspell: Yes I am. Bet you love it too
ashad04: Yes of course.
castaspell: ahh, I thought so
ashad04: You are endearing, like a little lost puppy that still never fails to chew up shoes even though it knows its bad but couldn't help it but is trying to get over it....
ashad04: But nevertheless cannot resist the siren call of the shoes...but not the pair of shoes...just one from each pair.
castaspell: Ahh...so I'm a little cute puppy now.
ashad04: Well at times...
ashad04: when you aren't rolling around in the mud
ashad04: then youre just a mangy little thign
castaspell: You know you lose points when you talk about me being mangy and your typing isn't as perfect pristine as usual. Tisk tisk
ashad04: Oh kiss my beautiful brown butt
ashad04: And besides cute or mangy, you can be such a little bitch sometimes

castaspell: oh I know.
castaspell: quite well aware :)
ashad04: As long as there is that.
ashad04: I gotta leave you in a few moments, tragic though to leave a patient in a vulnerable state.
castaspell: oh I know hunny, I am dreading the departure with bitter tears.
ashad04: You better watch it. You're a little too good at this...;)
castaspell: So would it count as one of my strengths then.
ashad04: Oh I would not go as far as to say that. It is an apparent inherent skill but not yet a strength.
ashad04: You must be able to demonstrate a mastering of it and responsible use of it before it is a true personal strength. Its just like all the other languages :)
castaspell: That's a rather fine line wouldn't you say?
ashad04: I would say. But I would also say an important line nevertheless
ashad04: and I might say "care for a snog," but I won't because I don't have breasts, so
ashad04: nevertheless I will leave you.
ashad04: and I thought of a good nickname for you so I'm going to start calling you DQ
castaspell: ahh...
castaspell: oh that's just great
ashad04: :)
ashad04: Will you be okay alone, by yourself?
castaspell: Eventually
castaspell: (tear)
ashad04: Never forget these special tender moments...
ashad04: passing through an hourglass...just like the days of our lives.
castaspell: Ok ok...gawd, just go already :)
ashad04: too far? Yea, too far. :)
castaspell: Goodnight Ashad.
ashad04: Goodnight Simon Drama Queen
ashad04: :-*

Subj:	**Jenn IM 6-19**
Date:	Sat. 6/19/2004 12:23:05 AM EST
From:	ssspellman@everydaysanctuary.net
To:	ssspellman@everydaysanctuary.net

Jennzen710: how was it?
castaspell: sucked
Jennzen710: y?
castaspell: got into a fight
Jennzen710: OMG how? with who?
Jennzen710: are you ok?
castaspell: yea I'm fine. the rest of guys found out about Ashad, called me a faggot
Jennzen710: um, so?
castaspell: dude it was messed up
Jennzen710: Its just a word isnt it? Just a fucked up word.
castaspell: yea they kept raggin on me then thou
castaspell: one thing led to another
Jennzen710: So let me get this straight…
Jennzen710: You didn't get into a fight because you had to, protect yourself or anything, but to stop them from teasing you?
Jennzen710: Hope Ashad doesn't find out what happened.
castaspell: WTF Jenn, why aren't you on my side?
castaspell: they started it.
Jennzen710: But did you finish it? Now that they know how to get to you?
castaspell: wait…hope he doesn't why?
Jennzen710: I thought you were fine with Ashad beinggay?
castaspell: I am. But I'm not like that
Jennzen710: Because, from the sounds of it, you didn't get pissed when they were calling him a fag, just you, right?
castaspell: yea
castaspell: so?
castaspell: but that's different since he is
Jennzen710: so, I'll say again, so what?
Jennzen710: and it doesn't matter if he is, that's still fucked up.
castaspell: so, I'm NOT
Jennzen710: soooo what is wrong if people thought that?
Jennzen710: What about being considered gay is worth getting hurt?

castaspell: It just is
castaspell: I mean if Ashsad is that fine but I just don't want to be, and I'm not and they kept calling me a fag too
Jennzen710: because you're hanging around with him?
castaspell: yea
Jennzen710: so they were calling him a fag?
castaspell: yea I guess so
Jennzen710: But that didn't bother you
castaspell: yea I guess not
Jennzen710: but then you got into a fight over that word because it was directed at you?
castaspell: yea, so?
Jennzen710: have you ever thought about how much shit he may get from being friends with you with some of his frieds?
castaspell: But this is different, what if they tell everyone back at school?
Jennzen710: what if some of his family or friends saw you two together, and started calling him a kike…
castaspell: DONTFUCKING USE THAT WORD!!
Jennzen710: and he got into a fight abou them calling him that?
castaspell: thatis SO fucking different
Jennzen710: how is it SO different?
castaspell: it just is.
Jennzen710: oh, ok. Just explain that to Ashad when you tell him
Jennzen710: that you got into a fight about being called a fag, not because they called him one. I'm sure he'll be able to understand that its SO different when you explain it to him.
Jennzen710: fuck it, I'm tired of this
Jennzen710: I gotta get up early tomorrow
castaspell: whatever
castaspell: fine, bye

Subj:	**liked you, lost you, loathe you**
Date:	Tue. 6/22/2004 3:40:52 AM EST
From:	rebeccaann88@everydaysanctuary.net
To:	ssspellman@everydaysanctuary.net

Simon, what happened to you?
Where did you go?

    My mind is downing in questions. I can't escape them. Nothing to hold on to, no where to swim to. And I can't make my feelings forget about you. Why did you run?
    Are you still alive? I know you are because I walked by and saw you working, but I couldn't make myself go in. What happened? What do you want me to do? We had a great time, and you said you would call me about the concert. Then the weekend comes and goes and no you.
    Why don't you like me? You sure seemed to when we met last month. And that night at your house. Then a good weekend. A good movie with a good person. An illusion?
    Why did you use me? Is this how you treat all the girls you say you want to be friends with? I really liked you. I thought you were a good person. I thought you would be good to me.
    I don't just do that with anyone... and now I have to think about you and that every time I think about those kinds of things again. I thought you were different. Weren't you?
    I thought you weren't shallow or dirty. If I wanted to get hurt I could have picked any guy. I picked you because you seem good inside. What happened to you?
    The you that was good will be missed. And the stupid part of you that is around now will be hated for making me

feel like a whore. And probably pity for all the others you will do this to.

Not the way I wanted to start my summer

I've never felt so special and then so disposable until I met you.

Thank you and fuck you just don't cut it.

Have a nice life.

Antiblog de Simon

6-23-04 1:25am

Why can't I be cooler?
It just seems like everyone of the fucking planet can go and do shit without getting shit for it.

    Taz is all about the lax bullshit like he's an addict and has two schools scouting him
    Travis is all smart and shit and has Brandeis as his fucking safety school
    Sanchez is going to join the army as stupid as that sounds but no one talks shit bout it
    And all the other guys have their shit together in one way or another

    Well and I guess there is Jenn and Angie who are kinda unknown what they want to do, but they always talk about their options and shit and make it seem so easy. And of course there is ashad with all the crazyass shit he gets into

I have NO FFUCKNG CLUE what I'm good at
I have NO FUCKING CLUE what I want to do!

AND I"LL NEVER HEARD THE END OF IT!!!!!!!!!!!!!!!!!!!!!!!!!!!!!!!!

    So I'm changing these to antiblog now, since its becoming a habit. I might as well have a real title since its my own outlet of bitching. Maybe then it will seem like it's a worthwhile way to spend an ten minutes at a time to keep me away from losing more friends by being me.
    Why can't I get paid for this?

Amd I might as well change fonts too...this isgetting looking stupid lieks it's a fucking assignment for skool

Hmm...I kinda like this one. ...will have to google it but I think it is one those French trebycapapult thingys...

Ohh yea, I'm going all medieval on your ass now! No simon no! NON!!

So ya I'm so cool now that I have a blog and I'm getting all picky with fonts.

Oohh...and I almost forgot! late addition to the wonderful world that is Simon's life

I WAS A FUCKING ASSHOLE TO BECKY AND I BROKE HER HEART AND NOW SHE HATES ME AND PROBABLY ALWAYS WILL AND SHE REALLY LIKED ME BUT NEVER AGAIN ND AND I"LL NEVER HAVE A CHANCE WITH HER AGAIN!!!

Way to go asshole
Just stick a trebuchet up your ass and be done with it

Subj:	**Sweet Diana IM**
Date:	Sat. 6/26/2004 10:18:24 AM EST
From:	ssspellman@everydaysanctuary.net
To:	ssspellman@everydaysanctuary.net

HotTamale86: Hey sugar

castaspell: Hola hotstuff

HotTamale86: hey btw, if billy asks, the story is weve never chatted online, and you don't know anything about him and me or even much bout me k?

castaspell: kay....

castaspell: ??

HotTamale86: long story...shits going down with us, he's been going all possessive and shit trying to tell me what I should be doing and that I should move out and move in with him and shit

castaspell: ah that sux, sorry sweetie

HotTamale86: thanx, no problema

HotTamale86: will figure it out

castaspell: so how bad are things

HotTamale86: ah he found out I still talk to my exbf steve and that been going out dancing with my girls and looking for anythin that looks like sthing to yell bout

HotTamale86: fucking stupid

HotTamale86: so hes going around suspicous with every1 i know

castaspell: well ill try not to look at your bum when he come in then

castaspell: well I already do, but you kno

HotTamale86: yea

HotTamale86: your cute

HotTamale86: this sucks. i luv him but he is just to much sometimes.

castaspell: well if he comes in ill just go off about asking out that dance studio chick that's hot and shit and make it seem like I don't know what an awesome setup you are

HotTamale86: **awwww**
HotTamale86: **no mas, simon your too sweet**
castaspell: oh thats only cause I cant have you,
castasepll: you were right…I freaked out on a friend again when she wanted to get closer
HotTamale86: **ahhh sorry to hear that**
castaspell: so yea, I'd somehow I'd end up fucing it up if you were dumb enough to wantme.
HotTamale86: **:)**
HotTamale86: **aw, dont say that**
castaspell: eh, tru do
HotTamale86: **well may be true but I do want you but I stay distant enogh so we don't mess it up**
HotTamale86: **cause I know your one of the guys the girls should want to end up with when they arent all crazy and and bullshit and shit. something the sisses taught me**
HotTamale86: **look at me rioght now i know bill is a dick, but I care about him and stick around and dont go for a simon thou cause ive messed up a cople friendships that way already ,like you**
castaspell: thats so fucked up though isn't it?
HotTamale86: **yeaa but thats the game**
HotTamale86: **hey hun gotta run 2 work, gonna be late!**
castaspell: aite, hasta amiga bonita
HotTamale86: **hasta amigo simon dulce**

Subj:	**Trace IM 6-28**
Date:	Mon. 6/28/2004 10:25:09 AM EST
From:	ssspellman@everydaysanctuary.net
To:	ssspellman@everydaysanctuary.net

castaspell: Hey!!
Trace08: Hey kid, whats the haps?
castaspell: Where you work again?
Trace08: near GovCenter why?
castaspell: I'm going down tonewbury with some guys to go to the virgin store was wondering how close it is to you.
Trace08: Oh a few stops down the Green Line. Think that's the Pru stop I think...?
Trace08: You going to come see me? :)
castaspell: nah, can't today
Trace08: ok,well just let me know, I can always get out for a few with the excuse of a coffee. Know how it is when you get the excuse to get into the city, like getting paroled for a day...have the same feeling living in it since I'm in this fucking office all time.
castaspell: thats cool
Trace08: actually, what are you doing tomorrow night?
castaspell: dunno
castaspell: working til 4, y?
Tracy08: if you want to, you're welcome to come this way for a bite, my treat, then you can root on me and my friends at our kickball game as BunkerHillCC. I have to get up early tomorrow so I won't be going out with them drinking afterwards, could give you a ride back.
castaspell: You play kickball? That is SOO weak.
Trace08: Right. I'm being told what is weak by a kid who is excited for the alien/predator movie?
Trace08: rrrright...
castaspell: yea bite me
Trace08: yea no thanks
Trace08: but the offers open if you change your mind. Could be fun, it's the playoffs so were playing two, and we're not playing the psycho team so we'll probably win
castaspell: what this is some kind of league??

Trace08: yea it's a sport/rec league...pretty good time for all of us indentured servenat office prisoners
Trace08: servant
castaspell: oh you poor thing
Trace08: oh shut up
castaspell: indent servant???
Trace08: yea like the whole colonial thing, binding work for years to pay for passage to the new world? You do still learn things in history class right?
castaspell: yea I guess I remem. That was 9thgrade thou, didnt pass, thanks for reminding em
castaspell: me
Trace08: you what? you gimp. Anyway, that works for all us student loaners. We indentured ourselves for college...our mid, and for some, their late 20s for our college eds. Sad how fucking much its gotten up to, don't envy you at all with that. Go cheap, go public if you know what's good for you.
Trace08: but hey, I gotta get back to work, so call me if you're gonna show up so I can tell you where we are etc k?
castaspell: k
Trace08: bye hun
castaspell: cya

Subj:	Trace IM 6-30
Date:	Wed. 6/30/2004 4:55:14 PM EST
From:	ssspellman@everydaysanctuary.net
To:	ssspellman@everydaysanctuary.net

castaspell: how'd the KB go?
Trace08: won one, lost one
Trace08: double elim playoff though so we're still in it
castaspell: right on,
castaspell: still think its stupid tho :)
Trace08: yea yea
Trace08: just give yourself a decade and you'll be yearning for a big rubber ball, you know it
castaspell: not that sorta rubber ;)
Trace08: one trackmind
Trace08: you're a sick kid, you know that?
castaspell: and? :)
Trace08: well in the fall if your not working too much and want to theres a dodgeball season starting up too   you said you liked the movie
Trace08: well you know what they say, 'admittance is the first step to recovery'
castaspell: who wants to recover?
castaspell: cool yea, dont know if i'll have timethou
castaspell: maybe next yr though after grad
Trace08: you always talk about wanting a girlfriend and yet you always play the fool don't you. Just be careful.
Trace08: I'll just say that it was alright with boys being like that in hs...but at some point make sure you get past it...I drove past my old neighbhood the other day visiting my parents and the same losers that were hanging out outside the candlesticks were still there I shit you not. Just with an extra 50 or 100 lbs
Trace08: promise me you won't be like that?
castaspell: what fat? no way in hell :)
Trace08: no, don't turn townie
castaspell: ah hell no, I'm getting the fuck outa here asap
castaspell: been looking into out of state schools.
Trace08: Really? Where are you looking?
castaspell: sticking with good sport schools pretty much

Trace08: oh please don't even pick a school based on that
castaspell: oh I won't, I'm not good enough to play hardcore anything, but just for the peeps and the fun
castaspell: been looking into the top party schools too :) :)
Trace08: You're hopeless
Trace08: You know your parents won't pay for that
castaspell: yea i know
castaspell: but yea, rents said theymight help wit outstate tuition if kick some asswith uping the grades and save upto cover the price of a umass theywill makeup some of the diff
Trace08: I think I understand some of whatever that was you just said..
castaspell: cool thou that theyve been cool with me going out to Amherst 'to get a feel for it' since they think I really want to go to school out there even thouh all I do is hang with with ashad and his mates and trying to scam with some sweet college girls and shti.
Trace08: well at least theres that.
Trace08: That's good of them for considerin it. Good luck deciding in the end.
castaspell: lookin for more hours at work instead of playing soccer this fall, so hopefully I'll have the $ by the end of school so can kick it for usmmer with the blokes
Trace08: happy youre keeping yourself busy though
Trace08: mates? blokes? You going british now for your next fad?
castaspell: nah I'm just down with some of the shit they say. I like mates and snogging and wankers and fuckalls and stuff.
Trace08: ok. well whenever you need a good kick in the ass to remind you where you come from think of me ok, I'm good at that.
castaspell: yes ma'am
Trace08: hey cut out that ma'am bullshit
Trace08: I know I'm older and cooler, but I'mnot ancient!
castaspell: haha yes, I know your good at that
castaspell: older yes
Trace08: ok better
Trace08: yea I was waiting for that one
Trace08: Alright. Time to get the hell out of here. Have a good weekend sim. Don't get into too much trouble ok?
castaspell: u2 bye
castaspell: always :)

Subj:	**Danielle...**
Date:	Thr. 7/1/2004 11:42:56 PM EST
From:	ssspellman@everydaysanctuary.net
To:	dscoleman@everydaysanctuary.net

Are you mature and respectful enough to be given someone's heart? Was it my fault or was it yours? Should I go celebat and stonecold so I won't have a heart to give? Was it my fault, did I have a choice?

Danielle, you holdmy heart as I gave to you. Somehow I saw my mothers eyes in you, but you hurt me so, my mother never did, and you aren't my mother, and you will never be her I know, but why was she so much in your eyes then? I wanted you to be, but you can never be in her shadow if you can allow me to be upset and you can't be wrong. I creid on your shoulder, how <u>nice</u> it was it felt so right, it was right...but where are we now, do you destroy what you helped let out? You told me everything was going to be alright, that it was ok that you'd be there. Did you know you were lying when you said that? Do you let it be, do you put up your vacancy sign and pack up? Do you come back to where you know you are wanted?
I gave you my heart and you accepted, we got upset and you hung up.

...

Paths always can cross

You said you think I'm special, well I agree.
You are special too, and although you tried and failed we are always together. A part of me in you, secret to most and the piece of you is starring at me from the inside everyday. What can I say, you get something and you gave me some. Is that all there is to it? <u>No matter what happens paths can always cross</u>. No matter where you go or what you say the paths you choose can always lead to me. I may waiver and I may distance but always know your in my sights. If you come back and I should not I will forever regret. You have a part of me and from that I will always know where you are

whatever mess of me there is is there for you to take,
simon

Antiblog de Simon

July 2, 2004 12:15am

Evanescence piss n moan

I couldn't stand this band when they came out. Just like Michelle Branch or Liz Phair.
Oh good, another fucking chick singer. Oh good, another fucking chick singer.
Except in this case cause they all are actually good. Goddamnit.

But there are still enough fucking fake posers to go around to bitch about
Fucking fake posers.

Must say though I like the idea of having these ABs having the potential of being clean cut with the spellchecky sorta thing, but there are just certain sentences that will unfortunately be greenlined like Fucking Fake Posers. Fragment, consider revising…um, no. That is a complete thought and is a complete sentence. About sums it up. thanks

So yea, I have to reluctantly to accept the fact that the cool chicks and their lyrics make sense, and in an actual real way rather thanthat fucking newlywedded nonsense shoved down your throat until you can recite it on command like it's a fucking pledge of alliegance shit. and I can understand that whole god pledgeallegence bullshit controversy every time some fucking snotty princess bithc at school looks at me like I just farted or told her that express went out of business when I tell her what an accurate opinion of Jessica simpson music really is.

What the fuck…why the hell does evan music have to apply so fucking accurately to me?

Fucking fake panzyass cocksucking cockteasing cunts. Another sentence that is perfectly fine the way it is, even if green and red lined across the whole fucking thing. Anyway, fucking look like skanks anytime you see them on MTV bitches and then you go pay a 100 bucks to look as much like them as you can. God, I had to walk through like a 100 prissy fake wannabe skankie popstars at Southshore, Taz and Chez and them were all like this one or that one were doableand ranking them and shit. Why? Because they have their tits all the way up and halfway out and their asscrack showing? You could stick a for sale sign in their crack that's showing. They all look like fucking manicans. manicans with fucking bad attitudes. Yea, I like boobs and butts too. But not when then encase a horrible whore of a person that just makes you wanna strangel someone, mostly them, but that would be bad cause you would have to go to jail for that so you bottle it up and hope for the Sox to win the pennet cause you know that that's the best bet since you know you gotta get a riot in. Fucking losers.
Hey! Can we nail some of you girls? Which ones? Oh it doesn't matter does it? Ya'll look the fucking same and have the same bitchy attitude, so can should we all just draw a number or do the pinthetail on thedonkey sort of thing? Yea, lets get back to our roots. Or we could all get into a great big fuckall mtvthemed orgy, but we'll do it in like the playgroud tradition...so how bout one girl one guy be captains, now pick. Gawd, it would definitely suck to be the last ones picked for this sort of game. Although suppose it will still be fun had by all.
As fucking sick, real sick not good sick, all those girls are, that would be a little bit fun. Game on!

Those fucking fake fools. Like this fucking Britney bullshit. Ashad all told me bout that this gay guy and chick who are reporters or something on tv married on protest of the fucking dicks like the paster at Taz's church who are all bigots bout the gays. They got married saying they hated each other and both have someone else and shit but they were able to get married cause their bodys could make babies. And then they stayed married just long enough to

beat britney and that fuckwit she waswiht for like a day.
Well it was a traditional marriage and they even beat out
popprincess. Cheers, now lets have some cake.
Thank you for flying Church of England, Cake or Death?
Uh, I'll take death if that otheroption is that fucking popcake
bulshit.

god i'm messed up
bithc about all the stipd bitches I see and Im about the most
empty and hollow halfwited fuckwit of a bastard.

well it looks like I'll be going with this antiblog sorta for a
while with everyone out of town or saying fuck off and all the
shit going down.   At least I sorta got tracy's sign of approval
way back when that I'm not totally gone for doing this shit..

I don't know what to think about all this shit but there just
seems to be something wrong with someone who doesn't
want to be called n*gger and who is celebrating a civilright
ani or whatever saying they need to stand up to fight to
protect people against people like Ashad. While I was a bit
uncomfortable around him for a while, he isn't exactly scary.
IT was kinda funny to see two little dudes on top of a cake
actually.
Yea here is where I feel better...trashtalking others.   So
fucking wrong...well though are you talking trash when your
talking about the oens that are the oens that throw it around?
Like all the bullshit of bush

BSBush with his whole,the people are not behind it bullshit.
Fuckyou! Fucking hicks in Alabama and SC aren't behind
it...so fucking what?!? fucking hicks in Boston for that matter.
A lot of em sure as hell didn't go for the no owning people
sorta thing, but they weren't given a fucking choice now
were they, because it wasn't right eh way it was.. And right
on they got bitchslaped. So don't give em a choice on this
one either. Fucking ass Fucking bigotBush. Oooo. I like that
one more than BS Bush. He's a fan of the nickname or initial

shit, So we'll go with BSGW Bush but really, BigotBush works on so many more levels the more he opens his mouth about this sorta shit but of course only until its too vivid then the oxymoron compassionate conservative card come out again.. Fucking trying to take George Washingtons initials. Jesus namedropping schemey BSass.
Then there's fucking Taz with his fucking faghating follower bullshit. Reciting lines like he's a fucking Hitler Youth. Thank god he's in Florida right now with all this going down, happy there won't be him and his loudmouthing on the 4th round here/ "those liberal activist judges, those corruptors of Americas youth, those special rights demanding fags" Do you actually think about what you're repeating wordforword from someone else before you say it? fuck. At leats they want to marry someone on purpose and just want to be able to do it like everyone else, which can't be said about your slut sister while you prolly follow inher footsteps and will knock some Natick or southshore mally skank up and have your parents force the fucking ankelchains on you to keepyou from runnig away but keeping you of course one of the saved cause you say you love Jesus and have the relationship blessed by god and all that shit and then you'll go on and wear a fucking wristband and then youll spend ten years paying off a fucking weddeing on top of the chick and the kidyou didn't even want cause you fancied a dicksuck and fuck from a dolledup deflowered sophomore for a night and who you ended up catching the eternitySTD all because you went for a piece of store bought calificationbeautification. Go Taz!
I wish he'd fucking opne his fucking mind sometimes. I feel bad for him though sometimes getting all that bullshit at home over and over. But at some point open up that fucking door to the whole thoughtprocess part of your brain rather than just retaining whatever the fuck you read in that focus on the family bullshit you have scattered round the entire house. How can you not see that as the propaganda t is. It is the same shit we learned from history class of the stupid shit pulled, ust with a fancier cover. Sad fucking pathetic scary psycho asshole motherfuckers. But really, what is so attractive about hating people you don't know so much, why...so you can play pretend that you're not in such a

shithole and being such assoles? And then you think Jesus loves you? You'd tack him up to a cross or Matthew Shepard him in a heartbeat if he was back doing his thing now and what could you do but say 'oopps' and you then have to audacity to blame jews two thousand years later for what a few people voted for back then, fuck you.
Fuckers.
Itd be cool if I could get him to be able to try and hang with ashad and his umass gang, get his mind off tits, lax and hs for more than five minutes. I'd fancythat. I fancy that word. Fancy.
And snog. Dude, snog is such a good word. It actually sounds like something you want even when you don't know what it is. Excuse me, would you want a snog? I dunno, what is it, is sounds interesting... oh, it is, trust me.
So I guessI can't blame Taz too much. And I won't give him too much shit when he gets back. And I won't give too much shit to the BSBush and crew forjust skating by in college and shit, I mean if my rents were all in the CIA and shit I'd be all buying up baseball teams and shit too, but, I mean comeon, at least buy a good one, shit. See what someone with talent can do with they buy a team? Hire the Pats front office to run some department, theres a Krafty owner who brings victories home and knows some fucking peopel That's fucking rad though the rangers are getting rad without arod...how bout a arod curse to trade off...upon the first full moon of the postseason a bakers dozen Yankees break bones within the confines of the Bronx and right before Boston comes for a visit. But Arod is still healthy. Well you invested in him so much so he could carry you right? Game on.
But still though...skating by a bit, cool...going awol and then deciding to have yourself a splendid little war with other peoples lives? What pisses you off so much that you have to kill people...that saddam and all them are better at it than you are? You would just love to use an Abomb wouldnt you? you convince everyone they have to do their bit in some mortal goodevil battle while you sit in the fortified occupied whitehouse and then you think you'll get up to heaven. You poor poor man....so lost. What is it, never could get any As yourself so you had to name drop daddy, jesus and the orig deadhead reagan to get a hold of some As finally? well now

you have shitlaods. have to admit it would seem attractive to me too if I always had a silver spoon in my pocket, and a silvermirror hidden somewhere and had no fucking concept of how the rest of the world operates of how to aquire your own silver spoon, so you just get a warchest and then boom, you got it going on.

 But really, where are all our own personal fucking water treatment plants and shit. You would just love to be able to throw your Agame around wouldn't you? As it is you try with little ints of bnkerbusterAbombs. You're like some person asking timidlyand quietly about an unclaimed dvd or something 'is thisanyones'? no...okay I'll juststick that in my pocket now... andthen get have a million people around the world helping you and unocal get its groove on in uzbekistan and some shit, but you can't get past the fact that you couldn't pick a fight and win against someone your own size. Its like your still in middle school. You're daddy could probably beat up anyone elses daddy back then being a real vet and all, and could torture and disappear him rather easily prolly by the time you were older, but you still don't know how good your Agame would be. You think you're big and bad. And you are. And you go after the easy fuckers like civilwared sandy countries. You couldn't go for a China. Oh you'd like to, you'd like to tell them whats up. You can't even take on a North Korea. Do you see how tiny they are? Coming from Texas that has to be bad on your ego, big fucking state you couldn't even avoid bankrupting and the ittybitty Koreans flip you off and you can't do shit bout it Come on, oyu have SO many more As than they do now! Why wait? But those crazy Chinese trapped your attenion telling you whatsup and shit with their whole lets get some sheshwan in space and shit. So all of a sudden you wanna go up on the moon again. I know what it is...you're afraid they'll one up you. You couldn't handle that, cause they're better at controlin and killing than you are too. So you gotta get up a plaque with your signature on it. And you know you got to cause if you don t they'll all go get up there with some of their Mao. And you wouldn't be able to handle that. knowing you won't even be able to get yourself on Mt rushmore so you gotta make sure that they don't make it Mao in the Moon. And dude, the Saturn shit is cool. Those fucking rings on the front page can captivate, but come on, we're all busy as fuck trying to pay for our Xanax and Prozac so you really need to get our attention with something that will last more than a minute or two. Sweet rings, oh a maybemoonbase but really we need another years dose of Fox. See you got the right idea with the xs and zs and shit for your drugs. Coke and pot and shit have all the boring letters. Not as good of scrabble potential when your on it. Gotta get the mind framed right. So fuck the moon shit, its amazing and cool to think about, but come on, you can't keep people's attentions with that when you're competing with Idol and idiots on mtv so really, we need something that will want everyone to flip back and be captivated by the war section of the paper. Yes, there actually is about a full official section devoted to it. See, you've accomplish something. But it is C- rate still though, but yourre on the right track. Just bring it home. Come on, get into your Agame, we need a good war on your FOXagra, so go for a pretty country. Yea! that's it! Fight the fucking fiji people! and, ... well you and fam already have florida locked up but its sorta likes its own country and its pretty so lets see some coverage, pick a few more little boys to go SWAT in and kidnap and you got the right idea with the whole inlimbo detetion bullshit but you gotta get that spiced up too and damn Ireally went to town witn those snekaing winecoolers tonight, but then what. Then what, oh and theres France but they're just sorta calmly comical, guess it doesn't all have to be dramatic, it can be like a shakspeare play. Gotta love the shit they still let us learn in hs eh? Yes, no child left behind, lets go for all of em! Hey, someday maybe you'll be able to go for a finland, but what have they done ot anyone lately plus their vodka bottles are pretty. You could always move onto Gs. There are a lot more Gs aren't there? Its like that crazy transy eddie said, the brits were just going down the line... they hated the french, then the germans and were going to add hungury, but then WWII, fucking Hitler had to come in and take the show, and then we took over, and really had the potential for following through after experimenting a couplehundred thousand yellowpeople bomb cause that is what it was right cause you didn't know of any Japanese, I mean you knew you only had three of em and you used them

all and those pesky japs still wouldn't surrender so you had to settle and go and clal your conditional surrender an unconditional one for show but at leat so the dman red wouldn't get all bigand bad and bring their army all asian too. So letters and colors I guess are what abombs are about. And yea without having to stop fucking five times a dayfor tea like the pomie bastards, wait sorry, Bass-tads, we really had some potential building right but really, its time to get moving in the alphabet, especially if we want to get that reagan apocelypse shit going on like I heard he was all about. Starwars? Ah come on that takes to long and its like , its like the mooshit...simplify, go with what you know works. Ffinding a group of people andcall them subhujan and then burn em up crispy. See andyou could get advertisers too. If its all about letters going then lets just start dropping those Abombs on all the Gs and Hs and Is and keep going. But wait, lets start with France, would be fittingly ironic since they are the ones that like playing with their As for no apparent reason on peaceful other letter countries beaches. Did you know pacific means peaceful?. Yea cool huh, anyway, at least there in pretty places non theless! See they are rubbing your nose in it too. Ok, so start with France...and just go down the list. A each country and by the time you get down near the end of the alphabet the 4 horseman would have to show up right? If not, we can just shrug our shoulders and say so long and thanks for all the fish, cause we'd probably have evaporated all the water so they'e be really easy to get and just sitting in the sun like the planet was just one big fucking ronco food dehydrator.
Alright, so Abombs for an Ahole that will help it get all the way from A to Z...the whole nine yards, all the way to the apocolyse. Oh I hope there won't be copyright probs putting Apocolpse Now on posters and in campaign ads? But you have the cash you could bythem all up for it oh and sit almost forgot about Arod. Hey why not lets have two fall curses show up. Never another yankee pennet winner in the fall and no more bushes bound for the white house after this trick or treating seasoin. No rings for Arod, and no Abombs for Ahole They yanks can be boys of summer all they want, but they'll just learn to take it easy in the fall, so come the last week of sept they just callup their tripA team for some big league

practice and some bad breaks. And the Bushes can be confind be bball owners and shit like that to their hearts content, just not from governemnetal offices. But they really should stick to the bad teams so we can root for the ones that will win. Or should we let them at leats have one divisional contentder? That would be fair.
Fucking A, i had a lot of coffee today
Wait...stimulant and depressant shouldn't that balance out?
Wow, the evan tracksafinished up a while ago and I forgot about the sorrowful attractive appeal of the wallowful depression and saddness for a few minutes, go me.

But of coursel'll replay them after I load up on some of that shitty bullshit bunny pasta wanna be macandcheese that the rents had to assault us with and fall asleep tothinking about putting a turnaquet around my heart for a few days, or a few years until the sox win it all,
so give or take a few decades
hmm maybe I should just senttle for a pennet too
hmmnm, valium could work. It has a v and it might actually make me sleep without a sever blow to the head.
Vs for everyone!!!!
Lets go rocky horror style and be done with it!

The title of this one should be... Evanescence piss and moan

Yes I'm really going now

Seriously

I really mean it.

Ilike that I do't need prescripts ffor my drugs. Caffine and catptured capecod alcapops
Ahhhhhhh....shut upsimon
And...…......................…...I'm
spent.

Subj:	**makeshift ab maybe**
Date:	Mon. 7/05/2004 2:35:20 AM EST
From:	ssspellman@everydaysanctuary.net
To:	ssspellman@everydaysanctuary.net

chattin online…can't be bothered with the dual comp thing…

The rents are letting me redec and paint my room while they are in redo mode…maybe it'll create a little peace around here, something we all have in common rather then the norm BS.
Aynthing I bitch about they bitch about me bitching about it.
Um…where is the fucking support!?? You have no fucking clue what I'm talking about,but you know what I should do and then you tell me you know whats important which never seems to be whatever is what I really am worried about…shocking no? why is it that post-hippies can be the most annoying OCDs?? Bitter bout giving in or selling out, have to take it out on the new wave?

Maybe I should hold off for while so I don't get all sadistic with black walls and spikey things hanging from the ceiling or something. Although should get the shit before they fucking find out about the fucking pike shit form that fucking cop from the other fucking week with the fucking ticket cause fucking SP have to be fucking assholes. Oh goodie, my winwage shitwork will go ot the fucking highway patrol. God idea, get a hundred bucks and create another masshole. Really iddn't have enough of em huh
Yeaaa…guess better not going around making too many decisions while in this pissy bitchy continual repeat of sad music phase.
Hunny, why did you pick those colors, you know those symbolize this and that and that if you really wanted to be happy and have the life I think you should have you should do the mamas boy motif approved by dr phil and then I won't have to snoop to figure out why you are al angsty and dark and I'll find your shit and get moritified that I did something wrong so I'll lay on some passiveveryagressive guilt AMAP…

Piss off NQMM

So next year…live with this shit and maybe pay no rent or cheap rent or go and live in an expensive shithole somewhere else and at least be able to be me, whoever the fuck me is or will be but at least it won't be a battle to just breathe…hhmmm

Subj:	**Trace IM 7-6**
Date:	Tue. 7/06/2004 3:40:14 PM EST
From:	ssspellman@everydaysanctuary.net
To:	ssspellman@everydaysanctuary.net

Trace08: Hey punk
Trace08: Long time no talk
castaspell: hey
Trace08: What's up?
castaspell: nothing
Trace08: You doing ok?
castaspell: yea whatever
Trace08: Ah that well huh
Trace08: Want to talk about it?
castaspell: not really
castaspell: everythings going to shit
Trace08: Like what everything?
castaspell: everything
castaspell: shit with the guys on the 4th
castaspell: shit with ashad
castaspell: and then more of that stupid shit with danielle
Trace08: What happened?
castaspell: dunno
castaspell: she just is being a bitch
Trace08: That sucks Sim, sorry
Trace08: Have you been writing any WTFs you care to share?
castaspell: no i havent i don't sorry
Trace08: Its okay…well when you do, by all means share :)
castaspell: k
Trace08: Simon speechless, what has the world come to
castaspell: yea i dunno
castaspell: its like i sent her this email saying you know i care about her and to not run away cause of some little problem whateva lets work it out, but she didnt even respond
Trace08: When did you write it?
castaspell: last thurs
Trace08: So it hasn't even been a week?
Trace08: You have to give her some time, its probably hard on her too

castaspell: yea i know
castaspell: just hard knowing she isnt in school, shes work a shitload but she has tiem for all the other shit in life and all her peeps but can barely seem send a txt you know
Trace08: yea I hear ya,
Trace08: In college once I had a boyfriend dump me, online, right before our class together
Trace08: and then the fucker shows up and just goes and sits with his friends like nothing happened, doesn't even look at me.
castaspell: was listening to ourfavorite song over and over as i was writing her that email
castaspell: and so i txt her the next day to see if she wants her cd back that it was on that i took to burn the song from and she just writes back 'no'
castaspell: i mean what the hell. You can't be bothered with typing more htan one word to me?
castaspell: is it that hard?
Trace08: Oy, that is brutal
castaspell: yeait sux
castaspell: i felt as stupid as the FUCKING cd
Trace08: You should ask yourself though would it really have been workable come september?
castaspell: then I heard she was all out at some show there with her frinds and her ex bf calledand she had enouhg time on her hands to talk with him for an hr tho
Trace08: Have you considered you may be better off without her?
castaspell: yea I know but we just had such a good connection. I mean I spilled my guts about my mother and shit going on with friends and stuff like that and she was all supportive and stuff and even hinted to me about some of the shit shes got about guys she'd had to deal with and shit and it was everything you always want with someone and then she goes spycho.
castaspell: I dunno
Trace08: Really? Wow. I didn't know that.
Trace08: Can understand a bit better why your hung up on her then. But more the reason she wasn't good for you if she couldn't handle that.
castaspell: yea
Trace08: Hope you don't let that keep you from opening up again when the time is right
castaspell: but how do I know when the time is right

castaspell: I mean this felt right and then its all messed up
castaspell: life sux
Trace08: Cant give you an answer to tha
Trace08: t
Trace08: sorry.
castaspell: its ok
castaspell: ill just go live in a monestary or something
Trace08: Dont say that
Trace08: You're so not the catholic type
Trace08: And you probably wouldn't last without girls
castaspell: yea your right
castaspell: but it sux
Trace08: Yea I know. i go into my I should be a nun phrases every six months or so if itmakes you feel better
Trace08: Depends on the guy though
Trace08: Sometimes its just that he's a dumbass and I have to slap myself for bad taste
castaspell: yea
castaspell: id rather be gettings slapped or shit than feelin this tho
Trace08: Ah hunny I know, I'm sorry
castaspell: its all good
Trace08: I once had a friend say to me that boyfriends and girlfriends are a lot like movies. And the reasons why some hurt more than others are that you realize that you just spent your money on this and it wasn't as good as you though it could have been
Trace08: The key being…'but there was so much potential…'
castaspell: yea
Trace08: just sucks that that pill is so hard to swallow
castaspell: yea i guess
castaspell: i should go thou, gotta go to work soon.
Trace08: Alright hun, you ok otherwise want to talk about anything else?
castaspell: not really
castaspell: but with a long night shift followed by the psycho am shit 2morrow it can only get better right?
Trace08: Ahhh, sorry si, well good luck with that.
Trace08: Feel better, write me or call me when you need me
castaspell: thanks
castaspell: and thank you
Trace08: Welcome, have peaceful dreams
castaspell: thanks

Subj:	**You Asshole!**
Date:	Fri. 7/09/2004 11:32:03 AM EST
From:	jennzen@everydaysanctuary.net
To:	ssspellman@everydaysanctuary.net

Simon, cut that shit out.
Seriously, lay off your bitching about girls in this or that and how you think they're all fucked up for one reason or another. You, can't fucking talk.
So shut the fuck up.
You talk with the same fucking tone as Tim its scary. The same fucked up televagnelsist shit, slaveowning sort of tone. You'd eb one of the fuckers that branded girls with big red As while your all tiptoeing around all free as a bird. You fucking asshole!!!
Do you know what I've fucking gone through to then have a "friend" come out with that shit? You disrespectful idiot.
Toothpick twats? WHAT?! You spent the time coming uyp with that shit and then thought to fucking to type it and send it to me?????? why, cause you got dissed? Deal with it you fucking cock...here's ones. Shitscared leghumping egotistical yesman hatchetman of a follower.
Not pleasasnt is it? that's whats being seen from the outside with this shit, but at leats I look inside and know what your all about...but guess you can't be bothered.
With all the poetnetial in you and you fucking piss on it.

Fucking assholes like you are like the sheriffs arresting women who get pregnant out of wedlock Becuaes it isn't "proper"
WHO THE FUCK ARE YOU TO DECIDE WHAT THE FUCK IS PROPER!???????
And then you go off on them looking like tramps or sluts or being hollow? WHO THE FUCK ARE YOU! YOU are the fucking hollow oen. You had 'fag' pretty high in your vocabulary for a while and now magically its gone but how dare those 'cockteasers'? Fuck you you fucking rotten egg. Been hanging out stagnant tfor too long in the basement little boy. fcking change with the seasons!

So what if they all change with the fashion of the week or month. Who are you to say what they feel inside? What about you? If you're a bit lost that's fine...but don't take it out on other people that are confused and trying to figure themselves out....this shit is fucking wrong. Making yourself feel better at their expense? What makes you so much gods gift? FUCK YOU

You're wrong Simon. You're WAY fucking wrong. I've been one of those girls before. So, how dare you, you fucking dick. For trying to say you're better than me, and then have the nerve to say you like knowing me and think I'm cool!! Fuck you!

`You're not just judging books by their cover. You're throwing them in a fire saying their worthless.You never even fucking opened them up!! I was one of those girls. I am one of those girls!!!

It isn't about the make up or the sunglasses or whatever the fuck else you call the stick up your ass and go round bithcing about Nooooo. its about you not being able to deal with you. Fuck you Simon. I've been there for you.   And then you go round using your shit as excuse to do the same like thm? Fuck you. Fucking WallBuilding Jew you are!
Asshole. Shut the fuck up. I should just tell you to fuck off once and for all andbe done with it, but for some reason I have to keep typing, to make myself feel better a little bit, so I don't write you off, so I'm no better you in that way and it pisses me off, but at least this isn't about anyone or any group of people, its about you, And I FUCKING KNOW YOU I went all alt and shit and it was the storebought version no better than what you btich about but wear at the same time, good one simon. Its all just different labels. I fucking branded myself with antibrands and thought I was good for a while.   It wasn't me. Its nobody! And its so fucking sad you can't see that. You worry so much about fitting in everywhere so you try to a little bitch to anyone set...but you flipflop so fucking much. you're a FUCKING EGGO! Only can feel better bout yourself by downing everyone else. WELL WHAT THE FUCK ARE YOU!!!!! Fuck you. You'd probably fucking kill someone if they acted just like you. You diss people who are as sad as you. HOW FUCKING FUNNY aYOU FUCKING REEK. Sad stupid boy you are.
    All the real problems in the world and have to create imaginary ones so you can feel like you

have your shit together? Fuck you Simon if that's who you're going to be.

Fuck you if you won't bother to look deep enough to see where I've been or where I've come from...you fucking....seriously, you bitch about Tim being stupid? Fucking shallowsurfacecritic freka fuck there are too many people like you in the world already, not going to sit around with you thinkign your so fucking cool or novel.

You're a fucking waste of time if you cant' see how bullshit you are with this shit.

You're a fucking waste of space if you can't get it

You're fucking hopeless if you can't take this If you write back ranting and bitchign, gop fucking delete yourself like you probably did this emeail.

You know you want to... delete this, say fuck that bitch and be done with it...be done with your life, be the bitter asshole already. Go for it

Or go tell that bullshit hollow asshole that is you right now to Fuck Off

You'll be all like, who the fuck does she think she is, all pretending to be all peaceful and zenny like that and then go off on th hat shit...

Well, you're an asshole right now and have been an asshole lately and here's your karma payback, bitch!

Dickhead.

Chickenshit.

I'm done.

Look me up when you get your shit together , hope for your sake its before a 10 year reunion or some shit.

Asshole asshole asshole.

Bye bye Asshole.

Jenn

Antiblog de simon

7-12-04 11:38PM

OMG, BookCrossing is so fucking cool!!! Some random person just up and left a book in the coffee shop this morning and I just stuck it behind the counter and forgot bout it but as I was cleaning up the counter cause it was Monday I had to pull it out and then and then all near closing I randomly check it out and there is a little id tag in it saying the person was all releasing it into the world to be found by someone.
Well right on. I'll be that someone.

Now where is the HotGirlDatingCrossing at? ☺

If I'm the god of hairdos,
Who's this god of books? No...wait...Goddess....oh yeaaaaaaa...

Antiblog de Simon

7-13-04 4:30pm

Just reading the first third of that shit left in the coffeeshop by that dude. I all went and checked it out online and just found this little blog entry on the book by some dude namd AJ. Thomas Paine Common Sense. I fished it out from under the register last night during the super Monday clean and just breezed through all background and intro today but stumbled on his bitch and moan of government. Seeing it as a necessary evil need to protect the people but not accepting claims of divine authority or whatever they all try to say is why their good or whatever. I mean I dig my ideas of what could be a good without the Bush bullshit of turning back time and having a groovier world dealio rather than the little clubhouse llike the UN...but would I I turn like into my parents towards trying to make kids almost skip adolescence because they've never left theirs? Am I favoring notions of something else to replace this BS that would be just as bad? Would I becomes just as bad with shit no better than what saddam or bush were or are trying to do? I mean they thought they were doing good shit right? Am I going all theotetcal right now cause deep down I know I'm full of shit? To make myself feel better since I don't know what the fuck is going on...?
If Jesus was a Jew and then later the Christ was tacked on him, and Paine was a Brit but American to later followers needing someone ot namedrop, what am I? I know what I'm not. Why am I so desperate for a label? Is it fallout from running away from the sporty and AE AE GAP follower factories? What factory have I run into trying to escape those?
But can I really blame all the ones still in there scared of turing into a rambly asshole loser that I seem to be? Gawddd.

Paine in my ass

Antiblog de simon

7-17-04 something 2am   another Friday night alone and at home after chilling with some television Rome, and an evening of Paine that sorta made me a bit more flooded but sane, and put me in a bit of a zone. Yea that sucked. No more rhyme attempts in the datings. Ooo... maybe quotes...? Wrote down a kick ass one the other day...

"And protest, only a bubble in the molten mass, pops and sighs out, and the mass hardens" - Shine Perishing Republic, Robinson Jeffers.   Dude!! The original American angster!

   So what hits me so hard in the 90s of Common Sense is the logic used against monarchies, that seems universal even today. But what really wack is the serious similiarity in these so-"american" principles, so well articulated then that totally bitchslap America today. They are totally "radical" ideas against this shit going on but are just watereddown as being the Americana shit or whatever. Common Sense?
   Well if we believe ducttape can save us from radiation, maybe we have lost it.
   The googinny on this Jeffers dude I guess that he was some bad ass poet was a founding member of the Cali hippie tribe type and all goes up and built his own castle, fucking rad enough right there but then was pretty much Galileoed after WWII for saying maybe peace is cool or something. Makes you wonder who is getting Galileoed nowadays. If Michael Moore and Al Fraken are still out there saying their shit, whoevers been silenced has got to be pretty badass.
   Galileo,Galileo would you please do the fandango?
   Hey Simon... ...coffee addict much!??!?
   Nahhhhhh........
   Wonder if there is a few century rule in the cards by the Bushes if they'll be a little better than the Catholic Church...although they steadily improved from where they were a thousand years ago but they are still at least a century or so behind the times. About as much as the pope is in checking out actually.
   Its all like the hypocrisy and the indignant happiness from those that go all Conservative Jesus worshipper kind of

thing - he was a fucking liberal people- or a America: land of the free home of the brave. You killed all the people that actually hadthose traits form the continent didn't' you?. And now "America" isn't even a fucking country, it's a state of mind that is being militarily focused down throats around the world like Walmarts, and at a high premium. Like Mass insurnce. A high premium for mediocre octane shit. probably leaded again too now that farmboy patterson checked out.

    Jesus, Mohammad, Buddha and any idolized figure that was 'radical' for saying "you can be better" and helping the ignored and mistreated are worshipped now, and their ideas are forgotten. Their messages are xeroxed but lose the context. Like Jesus and all his friends not being included in the category of Judaism. Like the fuckers that have the Proud to Be American bumper stickers and who don't contribute anything to making the identity like Ashad would say, so you are passive and ignorant but proud? Like a shitzu or some shit saying, I'm proud being the breed I am. Well what breed are you, what makes you special, what are you proud about? I don't know, that I'm a shitzu! Go shitzu! We're the best. Why are you the best? Umm...I'm just proud to be my breed. Well what have you done to be a good shitzu? ....I'm a shitzu! Go shitzus!!

    So fucked up. It's like the biggest thing this is as if its the most pornographic obscene thing, Janet Jackson had a nipple brought out. But politics that gleefully go for war? ...bit more dangerous don't you think? Oh shit, we are living in South Park, forgot, people don't think. And they all probably criticize South Park for corrupting the youth like its fuckin 21st century Socrates but boom, hello! Its too fucking accurate and true! Corrupting youth by what? By yelling BS?!? The whole point of playing BS or this life is to call BS on BSers!!! Go BS Patrol!

    Proud to be American though. Nipples are dangerous, not differing options. Not gay love. Love is love. Hate is hate. Electing leaders though to take us all to some concept of hell in some quasi holy kind of way with a President instead of a Caesar with the God Bless America bullshit stuck on the back of the motorcade as it heads at high speeds into hella bad hellfullness.

Do they ever wonder what it is God would want America to do? But the Bushes know, all assuming that they are his avatars or something and are divinely aware of his wishes and he wants whatever Mr oilman, lawyer, auto, airline, insurance, child laboring imperialist wants. Where's the logic?

Uncommon sense?

Galileoed common sense

Gotta go get my fandango on

Subj:	**Diana IM 6-21 Sexy!!**
Date:	Wed. 7/21/2004 12:49:22 AM EST
From:	ssspellman@everydaysanctuary.net
To:	ssspellman@everydaysanctuary.net

HotTamale86: **hola hottie :)**
castaspell: Hey gorgeous ;)
HotTamale86: **how are ya doing?**
castaspell: not too bad, and you?
castaspell: how was it?
HotTamale86: **AWESOME!!!**
HotTamale86: **wedding was beautifu, got a tan, went partying con hermanas**
HotTamale86: **(my sisters)**
castaspell: I know that one
HotTamale86: **ah good, youre leraning...**
HotTamale86: **maybe there is hope for you yet**
HotTamale86: **Thank you so MUCH for covering for me!!!**
castaspell: glad you think so, you should teach me some stuff
castaspell: ya no prob, easy for someone cool like you
HotTamale86: **oh, eager to learn are we, and so much trust :)**
HotTamale86: **I better keep my eye on you ;)**
castaspell: ooo, oh and teach me whatever you want cutie
castaspell: can i still keep both of mine on you?
HotTamale86: **I guess so**
castaspell: pref in the walking around in the rain with you in your white tanktop
castaspell: jk
HotTamale86: **oh no you didnt**
HotTamale86: **you arne't just kidding**
castaspell: noooo...you think?
castaspell: ;)
HotTamale86: oh **arent you just the naughty boy today**
castaspell: i guess so

castaspell: good thing we don't let the bfs and gfs know our passwords and shit huh
HotTamale86: yea
castaspell: makes you wonder what they may be up to thogh
HotTamale86: um yea dont want to think bout it
castaspell: k sorry
HotTamale86: its all good
HotTamale86: just a good thing thou
HotTamale86: especially cause I wanna hurt yu right now
castaspell: oh really? Please by all means. Wait, in the good way or the bad way? :)
HotTamale86: i can do both, if your good
castaspell: ok, wow. sure why not. What do I have to do to get both?
HotTamale86: now now im not going to make it that easy
castaspell: oh ok sorry
HotTamale86: you apologize to much
castaspell: sorry
castaspell: :D
HotTamale86: seriously, quit it
castaspell: seriously, ok
HotTamale86: ok, good boy
castaspell: oh so that's how you like it, being all commanding and shit
HotTamale86: you know it
HotTamale86: been trying to train the boy a lot lately
castaspell: must say im jealous
HotTamale86: of what
castaspell: of him being able to get boss round by you , id love that shit
HotTamale86: whateva
HotTamale86: actually your def hopeless
castaspell: so im told
castaspell: cant help it though, your hot, and you play back
HotTamale86: yea i guess i do
HotTamale86: damn
HotTamale86: ;)
castaspell: So sexy…you ever thought about me?

HotTamale86: **in that way? no**
HotTamale86: **but i could see you being being cool though**
castaspell: well I haven't tought about you either
HotTamale86: **yea right**
castaspell: yea I know :)
HotTamale86: **what have you thought?**
castaspell: oh just stuff
HotTamale86: **what kind of stuff?**
castaspell: just like what youd look like topless and shit
HotTamale86: **oh, thats boring, id expect that**
castaspell: would you be offended if I asked you a personal question?
HotTamale86: **depends on the ? doesn't it :)**
castaspell: well its fun getting paid to see you…but have eben kinda wondering like what your bra size is…
HotTamale86: **omg that is like so wrong and im so offended…**
HotTamale86: **jk**
castaspell: well…?
HotTamale86: **well what? ;)**
HotTamale86: **34C**
castaspell: nice
HotTamale86: **yea i think so too**
HotTamale86: **:)**
castaspell: now is when I'm jealous of your bf
HotTamale86: **why be jealous**
HotTamale86: **you get to see them more than he does even if you dontt get to touch them**
castaspell: yea I guess that is the glasshalf full sorta thing
castaspell: too bad we're not still in ms, id love to play Dr. with you :)
HotTamale86: **hey!**
HotTamale86: **actually you would have be a fun play partner I bet**
castaspell: wonder if they same would ever be true if we were ever both single and needin some at the same time
HotTamale86: **your too sweet to just use for 'some' but bet youd be fun to 'play' wit**
castaspell: WHAT??!?

HotTamale86: after you matured a bit
castaspell: hey
castaspell: whatdo you mean??
HotTamale86: well i wouldn't want to waste mytime with someone whos still a beginner and whod up and get scared when itd be a regular thing
castaspell: I wouldn't wig out
HotTamale86: right
castaspell: really, I think your hot and super cool
HotTamale86: then what about that girl a couple months ago you were with
castaspell: oh that was differnet
HotTamale86: ok, how exactly,
castaspell:: well she was just wierd
HotTamale86: well what if all of a sudden you thought i was weird? huh?
HotTamale86: i wouldn't want to let you see mi Cs and be mi especial without knowing you wouldn't go off and shack up someone else right after
castaspell: well hey you had that guy before this bf and you let him get you naked
HotTamale86: THAT was different
castaspell: oh now your with the thats different
HotTamale86: yea, cause it is. i didn't care about him. I like you Simon, and I care about you. And because of that I don't want to hurt you, and I know I could get hurt by you
HotTamale86: I know youd be able to hurt me since I like you, and right now anyway I'm scared you would. So I cant do that with you that hookup shit
castaspell: ah your so sweet, looking out for me
castaspell: and yourself (although I guess I cant blame you for that)
castaspell: :)
HotTamale86: yes exactly
HotTamale86: yea, so like I said when you all grow up then you may be able to come get some of this...
HotTamale86: ;)

castaspell: is that a promise??
HotTamale86: maybe
HotTamale86: ;)
castaspell: you are so evil!
HotTamale86: I know
HotTamale86: :)
HotTamale86: but you know you love it
castaspell: yea i do which is quite evident right now
HotTamale86: hey now, behave
castaspell: ok sorry
HotTamale86: hey and quit that
castaspell: ooops, my bad
HotTamale86: guess I can tolerate that...for now
HotTamale86: :-P
castaspell: so what you can tease and talk all sexy but cant hear about the consequences?
HotTamale86: nah I was just fucking with you, if I were being serious id tell you...
HotTamale86: if I were being totally honest I would tell you I wasn't exacty turned off by this conversation
HotTamale86: but i'm not going to be completely honest :)
castaspell: really??
HotTamale86: yep
castaspell: thats encouraging :)
castaspell:: would you be offended to know youll be in my thoughts for a few moments after we signoff?
HotTamale86: no not offended, more like flattered, but only if the thoughts are just the superficials that disappear with whatever you use to clean up after yourslf
HotTamale86: you've been cool enough in this chat i may consider going and doingthe same :)
castaspell: WHAT??
HotTamale86: shhhh, don't tell no one
HotTamale86: :)
castaspell: damn!!
castaspell: D, will you marry me?

HotTamale86: haha
HotTamale86: cute
HotTamale86: maybe, give or take a lifetime or two
HotTamale86: ;)
castaspell: ahhhhh :(
HotTamale86: don't sweat it sweetie, just playing
HotTamale86: who knows what the future may bring,
HotTamale86: def like having you in my life thou
HotTamale86: :)
castaspell: ahh...thanks
castaspell: same here :)
HotTamale86: see, nice to know
HotTamale86: but I really must be going
HotTamale86: so when do you work again next with me?
castaspell: fri i think?
HotTamale86: ok sexy, thanks ofr the nice chat...see you then
castaspell: no no no, thank you :)
castaspell: goodnight
HotTamale86:gnight
HotTamale86: wet dreams
HotTamale86: ;)
castaspell: :)

Subj:	**Hola and adios**
Date:	Fri. 7/23/2004 2:46:25 PM EST
From:	theigal@everydaysanctuary.net
To:	ssspellman@everydaysanctuary.net

Ok Si, so long for a couple weeks. I am going to be on a plane in just a few hours...Puerta Vallarta is calling...it says it was has drinking, dancing and debotchery available! There then LA to visit some friends! So peace out DNC, ya'll are cool, but I'm getting the hell out of dodge. This show my life for what it is...a spring break at the end of summer. Always late but never totally missing out right?! ;)
So, I'll be back the 2nd and I will be thinking about you. Just think, this time next year you could pop yourself down there too

Trace

Ohh, almost forgot, I heard this and had to relay...a super funny story that might cheer you up for a bit...I know you'll appreciate it in some way.
So this friend at work coming on the trip with me was over at my place while I was packing and had just had gotten back from visiting her friend in NY on a business trip and that friend works at company where this whole thing originated, and so here is how the story goes... so there is this woman working there, from India whos name is anjalie or something but spelled way different than you'd think and so their boss sends out a department wide update memo apparently clicking the default auto-spellcorrect. Well, instead of saying how this person is working on this project and Anjalie is on top of some other project, the spellcorrect made it "anal," throughout the whole email!! So I guess throughout this whole email sent to the whole deparment it was anal this, and anal that.
So hilariously the response comes from her, replied to all in the same professional memo format even with one of the Re: subjects. -Let it hereby be known and please update your programs accordingly that the employee working on so-and-so project is named Anjalie, not "Anal." Please correct all auto spellchecks, thank you. That is all.

that could have been one of those "priceless" commercials definitely.

Anyway, I'll be coming over when I get back to chat with Janice about new job options...so see you in a couple weeks!

Antiblog de simon

8-12-04 11:45PM

      For shits and giggles just did a craigslist personal ad. And of course, WTF must be asked...who am I? It prolly sounded really lame. At least no one knows your address from it thou. Had a thought thou. To find the right person. Should I just lay it out with stupid references and tell people to respond if they get em all...who can know me without knowing the merits of Stewie and Stan,
      Shit, how many times have I deleted paragraphs or full abs cause the fuckers start sounding like I'm writing it to an audience...editing myself from myself...good, simon, you think you'll get a girl when you can't even get through a first date with yourself....hey!!!!!....

      "I think I've learned something here today. It isn't a matter of what you write or what you reference...but why you wrote it or referenced it that counts. Don't do it to feel smart or wit it. ... Ah, yes!... Victory is mine!!!!!!!... no.... wait...

DAMN!!!!!!!!!

The man in white? Yes, it was the man in white. It couldn't be me, well this me. Cause the whiteman me wouldn't be writing this. Where did he go? cartooned caffeinated postwork simon is when the brainwashy whiteysimon sleeps. My ego is white. That is the part that is lilywhite and can't handle looking stupid so it disses the world. Finally, I get it!

But...How much longer til my Stanlygood, StewielyCapable self is able to destroy the Man in white self? Seems like they can walk and use their opposeable thumbs but still not ready for the coup de simon, maybe just a bit longer for finemotor and engineering skills to build that handy ray gun.

Ok Stewiesmoothbutnotevil self....how to save and title this entity so as the man in white may never be the wiser?????????

Weebles and whores?
Wine bottles and weed?
The best boobs are the ones not overly bound or recently bought?
Big boobs are better when not bought?
Oooo....

The best boobs are not bought...
Or...
The best boobs are actually breasts

(Thanks Trace) ☺

Best boobs are actually breasts

Subj:	**to be antiblog**
Date:	Wed. 8/18/2004 1:48:49 PM EST
From:	ssspellman@everydaysanctuary.net
To:	ssspellman@everydaysanctuary.net

I can't believ this shit!!1 Why do I have to choose which friends will stil be my friends? Why can't it just be that everyone gets along in a crowd? Fucking A it's a crowd for a reason
Best friends since fourth grade shared so many memories and experiences and now may olose it because of someone else that want sto be my friend? Because he likes boys? Why?
Why why why why why why why?????????????????
Everyone is good, I know that, and then everyone has something wrong with something about me and makes it the end all. And I wonder why I'm lonely sometimes. No one is happy with me.
I'm sorta happy with myself now, which is weird. and then is when this shit hits. What the fuck?

I don't know.

When Everclear and Guster make sense in life you know you got some shit to deal wtih.

"You do what you do, you say what you say, you try to be everything to everyone. You know all the right people, you play all the right games. You always try to be everything to everything. And you do it again. You always do it again."

Hope and await for a day when that doesn't apply to me with friends going unfriends
At least there is some literary/lyrical support

"Say goodbye, lose your friends, make them go, don't need them around, cause its time lose your friends, make them go, was never suppose to be like this.
Go on, if this will make you happier, its got you this far, do what you have to

You've wasted every moment of your Saturdays, and your Sundays…and like your father said, just do what was done onto you."
… and so you do.

Well not anymore.
Goodbye Tim. Look me up when you have your Taz tamed.

Subj:	**Trace IM 8-23**
Date:	Mon. 8/23/2004 8:49:05 AM EST
From:	ssspellman@everydaysanctuary.net
To:	ssspellman@everydaysanctuary.net

Trace08: hey punk
Trace08: What are you doing up so early?
castaspell: hey girly, whats cookin?
castaspell: got the midmorn shift and trying to get normalized for skool
Trace08: Not to much, aiming to get enough done to get fri off so been here for a couple hours already
castaspell: don't envy you
Trace08: So have you peaked at that book yet?
Trace08: yea don't emulate
castaspell: yea, trying to get through it actually before school starts up again, been getting through some serious shit lately…maybe I should save some of it though for comic relief later.
Trace08: Yea its good for that huh
castaspell: must admit, I just took it to shut you up…
Trace08: Well I'm happy you did anyway
castaspell: but it gets good quick. I liked the reality rearranging mockingbirds a lot and have gotten to the philosphizing (sp) can of beans so far, and the weird ass turkeymobile and the sexcrazed couple.
Trace08: I knew you'd like those. And hey, some new heterosexualing, wasn't that was you were looking for? I actually decided to give it to you from something he says early on in it. About lack of articulation being the onset of mental illness, thought of you with all the people you have to be around at work and at sociopathic kids at school. :) So you don't go stupidly crazy.
Trace08: Wasn't that nice of me?
Trace08: Yes tracey, that was really sweet of you, you're so kind.
Trace08: Ah, yes I know I know. I do what I can
castaspell: yea yea yea, you are gods gift and all of that
Trace08: Oh thanks for noticing!
castaspell: cheers to that!
castaspell: can your cans do any tricks?
Trace08: Watch it bud, or I'll tell your mommy :)

Trace08: (eve if stepish)
castaspell: but I thought you were gods gift?
Trace08: Well yea but just as so many of God's gifts, this one can't be quickly or fully understood by humans
Trace08: Or even seen in their natural state by impressionable minds...
castaspell: ahhhhh :(
Trace08: Ahhhh...it's so fun to torment you.
Trace08: Just like the good ol days
Trace08: We had fun didn't we?
castaspell: what you mean like when you dressed me up for your fashionshows???
Trace08: Oh my god!!!!
Trace08: I totally forgot about that!!!
Trace08: How do you remember that?
castaspell: well it haunts me in my dreams nightly...
castaspell: yea I found some pictures in some box somewhere...
castaspell: which have since been unfound...
Trace08: Ohh you have got to let me see them!!
castaspell: Ohhhh...NO
Trace08: Ah hunny I'm sorry about that...
Trace08: But you were so cute! :)
castaspell: don't know if I should take that as a compliment or an insult.
Trace08: Oh stop! You used to torment me too when you actually got old enough to fight back
castaspell: Yeahhhh
castaspell: :D
Trace08: Ok so its all balanced out then.
castaspell: except for all the years of therapy I'll need
castaspell: but whats that anyway
Trace08: Oh shut up
castaspell: :)
Trace08: So you ready for school?
castaspell: a big hell no is the usual answer...but actually I am looking forward to it for some stuff. Not looking forward to seeing a few people round there though
Trace08: really? like who?
castaspell: well you know, al the guys like Tim if shit gets started again. Hey Trace, can I ask you a ?
Trace08: Sure. Go for it...

castaspell: Can I call you and ask you for help for a email to becky
Trace08: What, so I can help you hurt her again? Sometimes you just got to leave things alone Sim.
castaspell: No no, a I'm sorry I'm such a fucking idiot sort of thing, like if I wrote it up and sent it to you, would you edit it for me or something?
Trace08: I suppose, I'll look at it for you. But no more womanly wisdom :)
Trace08: So are you going to follow through with your sport decisions?
castaspell: yeah I think so
castaspell: who knows though
Trace08: Good for you
castaspell: not having worked out in a couple months helps that work itself out though :)
Trace08: But you've been skateboarding and stuff right?
castaspell: oh yea but I all mean the hardcore stuff. But yea I still tool round town alot
Trace08: Well see that's good. I hardly have time to do the gym most weeks
Trace08: I can get myself out to do it in winter but not the summer for some reason.
castaspell: yea, youre so messed up
Trace08: Bite me sim
castaspell: ok!
Trace08: ehh, not like that!
castaspell: haha, you're funner to tease!
Trace08: yea yea well I better get going so I can get outta here
castaspell: miss me :)
Trace08: Always do you little tool
castaspell: :)
castaspell: thanks again for the book
Trace08: no prob
Trace08: Keep working on it and maybe someday you'll be a decent catch, in ten or twenty years
Trace08: ;)
castaspell: just like you
Trace08: ahhhh
Trace08: Lookin good so far
Trace08: Byebye Si
castaspell: bye babe

Subj:	**you sweet sweet boy**
Date:	Sat. 8/28/2004 1:36:04 PM EST
From:	theigal@everydaysanctuary.net
To:	ssspellman@everydaysanctuary.net

Damnit Simon, you asshole, you made me cry with that card.

    I'm sorry I've been so out of it and so negligent these past few weeks as you're no doubt stressing about deep things too. I trapped myself in some bad patterns and lost myself in a lot of work. No excuses, just explanation. I was putting projects and timesheets ahead of the important things.

    But know that I'm in at work right now for only one reason. To write this to you.

    I didn't even know you knew it was my birthday, I always knew yours was two months after mine, didn't know you had the inverse down. Okay, work words are coming into this (consequence of being in this building I'm afraid), so better stop smalltalking, because it feels like I have a lot to say to you.

    You hit me with what you wrote, and I appreciate it. It was like getting hit deep down by a big bear hug. There was so much worry and fear in your words at times and I am so touched that I am so important to you through all that.
    So in short: You're welcome. And no problem. And thank you. For letting me be there, and wanting me to be there.
    And in long: You're doing so well, and don't sweat too much....its a long road and often a tough journey, but it's everything that matters and more, and that's what makes it magical.....and you've been teaching me that this past year little bits at a time as much as I could be to you (and you didn't even know it).

    I'll probably go too la-la for you in this, but oh well...seriously Simon, as you are wanting to work through this stuff in this tough part of life, its just a little tiny change or two that can make the biggest difference. You just have to view, and I know it's hard of course since you are still in the middle of it, but just view your life as a little minuture world and see that its okay that you can't make everything smooth

because you want to. If you did you wouldn't have any land to stand on and you're still a crappy swimmer right? So there
So just realize that its okay.
See it's like this...... you have to view where you are in the thick of things from outside the thicket. Oh, impossible you say? I say, you lazy sack of shit, use your imagination!! :) But seriously......just look at where you are as not being so pressured like it's a timed exam or something. Seriously little bud, adolescence is simply an annoyingly concentrated manifestation of the universe and everything that it is, encased within a life stage probably for the eneteratinment of someone. So for the rest of our time here with struggles and fun just realize that through each day we're just in the midst of something huge. Its hard to se sunrises and sunsets a lot around here I know, but try to just imagine that sort of feeling you get when you see one of those suckers....that you can't comprehend it all even as best we try. That's the little shooting star version of feeling divine or whatnot.
You know that bit about high school being that thing that you spend the rest of your life getting over? Well, in general it is a hint of a secret to life I think. Its like this.....adolescence or whatever is that intense shit you have to go through is that blinding view of what everything is all about. And everything past it in your life is just a chance for you to live through it, and try to live with it, rather than trying to exist on in spite of it. It's a concentrated, potent, intensified for your enjoyment, view of life and all the possibility in it. It's a view of God, Goddess, the God Family, the Divine, whatever.
Like how space and time curve and warp and are so damn complicated...so is life, and you have to just understand you are forcibly, and if you want to learn and grow past it, must accept reluctantly, is "you" right now. You have no idea how long it took me to even have to confront that let alone accept...the thing that in the end you realize though after fighting it for so long is that its all you'll always be unless you work for it, for more to the story of you. Don't become a past-its-prime sitcom or something. Work with what you're dealt when the cards are out, but don't be afraid to reshuffle and learn some new games when you've mastered this or that and things change up.

Remember a while back when I mentioned about seeing those twits I knew from high school outside the alley who couldn't recognize me but they looked identical?
You have to accept that that you should change. Puberty kicks the shit out of everyone that goes through it. But the thing is you can't have all the good parts of you inside go run away and hide forever, because eventually the storm dies down, but you have to rebuild. Puberty is like a decade long series of storms and disasters waiting in line, cloaked so you don't know what is next and just when you have rebuilt and even strengthened yourself against some of it, the little grin

that you can only imagine God or Whomever having when you have to have a new something come up and knock you down and then bite you in the butt for good measure but nevertheless the thing you need to be exposed to, need to learn to weather.

You're forced to confront yourself...face to face. It sucks. I know. I have never really gotten into things with you into much detail I know about much and then I ttry to go all deep but with gerenal things and it doesn't work well...but I can feel it pretty safe to do so more lately seeing how youre weathering these storms lately, so here goes a little opening a sweaky old door in me.

I've only come to where I am at now because of some serious motherfucking hurricane punches that come in to shake you up like 10.0 earthquakes with the wipe out power of a tsunami. I had to meet myself face to face a number of times, and each time had to retreat, scared at what was seen from all those different angles. It freaked the shit out of me. I know you have nearly shitted yourself a few times lately.

In the end, you just have to accept that it could have been better, it could have been worse and in the end, it may be either way as we go on in the future, and will probably be both, with a grin. :) But how they hit you and what happens through them is up to you.

Okay...here it goes...

I was molested. It isn't important when or who or how...only that I was. It was...and for so long, it was *me*. I completely was that ugliness and hideousness. I hated it. And I hated myself....... It defined me. It confined me.

In the end it suffocated me. And in that forced, and humbled way where you realize "you" didn't help yourself out of it so much as you were removed from it all of a sudden and suddenly you're away from it, I was almost magically face to face with myself. That's the first time I met, for lack of better descirption, God. Whatever pointed out the way out, I ran out of it and away from it so quick and so fast I didn't know where I was with anything. I don't know how. But, sudddenly I found myself staring at myself.

That horrible, dirty "me" was running because it was scared to admit what it was - at the same time graced by the right looks and imprisoned by the assaults against me that those looks were blamed for- talk about the worst kind of Catch22. So I was suddenly contronted. That me that I'd known was eye to eye with the fragile and tender creature that was the soul inside that sadistically tattered and tortured vessel. So it was magically that they swapped features and yet they felt the same. It was all me. Pretty but empty. Ugly but so full, and so beautiful. But at this awakening, the only me that had any control then, that I knew of anyway, ran away screaming...that is the only way I can explain it. Unable to accept there was anything good inside of it, it fought. Up until then, it didn't have the ability to know anything nice and good without having to hurt it so it was okay that it would hurt me.   It took ever more intense and confronting times like that before I accepted them. And only then did progress start and did it start to smooth out.

I am sorry that I can't explain it but in abstract like that, but I hope you can understand it somehow in some way. It took me so long, and so much, to be able to come to terms with it, to even admit it to anyone, and so so so long before I could admit it to myself.

Don't know if you would remember the boyfriend I had many years ago, Keith? He was dismissed at best as a "phase" etc by my family and criticized by so many of my so-called friends as a loser of one type or another which I won't go into, but he was the first person I ever told.... he was that special person because of all the sides of him that he allowed me to see, looking back I can't believe that he could have been so secure like that...... and because of that it was he actually who was able to help get me to be able to admit it to myself, the person who helped me meet myself in a sense, and to be able to be kind with myself.

You never know how similar, or how connected we all are, until you knock down those walls around the good parts of you you create to contain it. There are a lot of specifics behind that anyone's closet of skeletons you can never know, but which I want you to be able to at least feel mine so you realize its all the same closet sort of thing.

The real you, your soul or whatever, can weather it all, that's where its from, it is the artificial parts of us that we create, ego and selfconscious aspirations and worries, (just rerealizing that myself after months of forgetting in this job) that are vulnerable to the elements. Don't contain yourself up in a self-made prison like that. That building is the first thing to go and it'll collapse all over the good you if you're not careful. I've learned that that's the only inevitability in life if you go down that path. I know so many people, around me on a daily basis that do it still, and who feel nearly hopeless with life, who never will get out of high school in their hearts. It is so sad.

You can't control the weather. We can't control who we are and have to work with what we've been given. It took me so much longer than it has taken you to realize that. I don't even think you know yet that you have realized it. But you will. So I say what I do to you with that in mind.

Through all the storms you'll go through, please learn to weather it all and build better and let your soul emerge and...well, just don't rely and demand the world to change for you like those who have lost their souls from their own devices and who contract out their building and supplies to too-good-to-be-true deals. I heard someone say that once somewhere, and I can never help repeating it. Never put all your trust in infomercials and never make a lot of yourself dependent on used car salesman-like person for approval

Simon, I love you. I see so much of myself in you. That me that I met only in these past few years. And it helps me a lot, so often, and it is so funny you never knew that until now, and only after you hit it with that card without knowing it. And that you have that in you and you have touched that in me is what makes me feel magic still exists in this world…… that if what is so special, what is so special about you, can be in me, then that there is no way we can totally extinguish it, as long as we are able to really remove peek outside and breathe deep,, that we can be better.

It simply is this Simon, You only can genuinely gain that calmness you are seeking when you stop hiding from yourself each time you're confronted with it. You can't go looking for it, trust me, I've tried, but you need to work on yourself little bits at a time so you aren't as freaked out when it happens. And eventually you will figure out what it takes for it to happen.

You know in dreams when you are in school naked or running from something that isn't on slow-motion like you are? What is really going on is a part of yourself training itself little by little when the active ego high school "you" isn't bothering it and getting in its way. Get yourself to a point where you can meet yourself and, however uncomfortably, be able to say hi. Eventually if you work for it, you will find yourself saying hello to yourself without fear and with a hug and a smile, losing track of the differences between and only seeing a bunch of equally non-threatening yous, all just hanging out with each other, just all you, from different angles. And in the practical way, that is truly when you know you can "know" other people on the inside.

Okay, I'm probably going a little too far for you too fast. But it is just this: the peace you seek and the happiness you strive for, are yours and they are everyone's at the same time, so you aren't alone, and you are not trying to figure out something impossible or in competition. And it is only in the pursuit of that it becomes "visible" Only in the babysteps does the horizon actually "come" to you…because you came to it.

Give yourself a hug and a kiss and smile from me when you meet him, okay? And the next time you see the sun moving in the sky, think about all of us busily doing that rotating around it, that we are a part of the magic that makes it light us up, day after day. okay?

You are beautiful Simon trying to learn to swim and anxious to get out there and be a part of that great big ocean of Awe. It makes me smile.

Happy unBirthday little buddy..... be well. And be you.

with affinity and awe,

Tracey Elizabeth

Antiblog de simon

8-30-04   1:00pm

      With all the don't know whats going ons with me, I figured I'd make it even more complicated and confused...so finally saw Passion.
    Was against giving Mel five bucks, but wanted to see it so I could know it or get a reference to it...so went the roundabout friend way of it.
    Dude, that shit is fucked up.
    Way bad, way awful what happened...simple as that.

Pause...

    But...um...what about the Romans? Where were they? I'm all with Eddie on this shit, like they were like Brits in Saving Ryans Privates or something, in the background...a sprinkling of them on top after alls said and done, made and baked. Every time the shit would be coming down on "Him" though I couldn't help hearing Ashad in my head, something he was telling me like a month ago bout the shit that went down in Iran back in the day. how can Americans identify with Jesus and the not-even-around-yet "Christians" more than the Romans when they are the ones putting up puppet leaders around and going all empiring and shit and willing to kill to keep the power, but at the expense of losing the soul or something like that.
    Those 'dangerous liberal sandy bass-tads'. Hmm...though wasn't Jesus a liberal sandy bass-tad? Go liberal sandy bass-tads. Dude, if Jesus was a teacher, he'd be the doctor who'd insist on no one calling him that...you could noncapitalize his name or forget ti turn in an assign like I do and he'd be all cool as long as you were being all cool and giving respect to everyone.
    Well I'm going all biblical and my typing is actually not going at full rant speed. Suppose that is a good sign. Don't

know of what. But there is definitely not as much green and red going on up above.

I have no clue what's the dealio with all the shit around like the GOP going all RNC in NYC and pushing the 9/11 buttons each chance they get like it's the applause sign for an old crap season of SNL, and then saying God this and God that...trying to play both sides a bit yea? Empires and the Eternal? Not good bedfellows are they? They don't really mesh well...like Saddam and Satan.
Who's my creampuff??
Yes, like so much else, it does come down to that.
Why is it you can't show war footage that is real, right now...but you can redepict it and get compliments and awards for the realism you correograph to show...as long as it is in a movie. I don't get it.
Does anyone?
I don't have the patience to figure it out and and if I don't have enough to care about that than how am I going to do this year...but whatever but I'm not really in the mood.

School starts soon. And I don't know how its going to be. Who am I going to hang out with? What am I going to do?
I'll be working a lot and studying a lot if I can transfer up levels, but I'll also be staring at walls in my dark room alone a lot I bet. A lot. A lot. A lot. A lot. Yeaaaa...need a littlehelp.

Dude, music gets really tweaky when you start thinking about the lyrics back at youself. And I've been thinking it about me...me singing it, it being me who its about...and its Third Eye Blindy and don't really know what that means but...its all a-la Tracey like I'm kerokeing to myself in case a self or two happen to be passing by

'I wonder hows it going to be when you don't know me . Hows it going to be when you see that I'm not there. Hows it going to be when theres no one there to talk to...'

I gotta this shit out in me, so the better bits of me don't say peace out asshole like what I've heard lately. Fucking hell.

Passion and dispassion

Subj:	**sorry becky backup**
Date:	Tue. 8/31/2004 2:15:33 AM EST
From:	ssspellman@everydaysanctuary.net
To:	theigal@everydaysanctuary.net

Rebecca,

    I don't know what is making me write this, and I don't know even if I'll send it, I'm just typing in the computer trying to find a way to say somehow in someway what I guess could be said with saying I'm sorry, but which doesn't seem enough.
    I'm sorry for hurting you.
    I wish you would have hurt me first.

    It's this simple. I can't see it going any other way that one or the other. Considering you are just too amazing. You're beautiful, nice, sweet, smart, considerate, compassionate, and just a little bit sassy. And well. I don't know, but its like that cliche which unfortunately rings true now...be careful what you wish for. I've wished for you for so long. And after all that time, it's only when you show up that I realize there is no way I'm ready for you. I just got dissed in that same fuckedup deep way though. Sorry, it doesn't matter about that, but simply though, those unwanted psycho feelings I had from that made me realized you must have had. And I am sorry that I caused those. Does it make you feel better though if you knew the girl I got burned by this summer Simoned (American Idol Simon) my heart in even a more messed up way than I did you? Probably not though huh. sorry.
    Why does it take shit like this? I didn't even think about how wrong I was, just disappearing and then up and emailing what I did after your texts and thinking it was something good to say....I didn't see what the fuck was the big deal in what I said to you until Laura came up to me at work last month and said, "shit that was fucked up...what you said to her"...I was like "what do you mean?" and she was like, "telling her

straight up she was nice and cool but basically just not nice enough that you found someone better." Yeaaaa...and then in the process letting slip some stupid little names, dates and, places making your head and heart add them up. I'm sorry.

    Why can't we fast forward so we don't keep fucking shit up one hour before we wouldn't have...fuck I'd settle for 5 minute speedup...it feels like it was sooo long ago that things between you and I got going...but it feels like it was just last week that we had that end all bitchfest. I don't understand that. Why do some parts feel fresh and some stale, and all the while, I can't escape the fact that the idea of you, the feeling that I get when thinking of just you in my life doesn't feel like any of it. And for that I made you cry. I wish I could have been burned by Danielle before I met you, then either I wouldn't have dicked you over, or I wouldn't have tried with you and maybe not ending up losing a friend. A friend I'll be sad to have lost forever if not able to come back from those bad experiences.

    I felt so safe and free around you. And I loved it.
    I feel so young and stupid with the thought of you. And I hate it.
    When we were just hanging out or screwing off it is so cool and I can't figure out why. Whenever shit goes down at home or there were fights going on for no good reason I craved to be around you.. And you are so amazing, and you are around and I could have had you, but then what do I do, something...anything...to push you away. I pushed everyone away lately, but none worse than you What's wrong with me?

    I started my journalthing again. But I kept stopping because it sounds so Gdamn stupid. So you get the shit end of that too since all this shit is coming out in the letter to you. I don't even know if I should send it. I'm just saving it and editing it so if it does go to you it won't have any of my stupid shit in it...cause well, going with that whole playing catchup thing...I'll make sure I read through it a few too many times before I send it to you.
    I know you hate me for disrespecting you. But would it make a difference if you knew I hated myself for that too?

But one of my favorite songs I've been listening to nonstop for the past couple days, Everything you Want by Vertical Horizon (I know I'm such a tool). "Now you're here and you don't know why. He's everything you want, he's everything you need, he's everything inside that you wish you could be..." (gotta love winamp for the scanback so you can recite lyrics to someone special in a somewhat special email that you might send... Anyway, but yea, change the hes for shes and it hits a nerve. I think you know where I'm going with that one.

But yea through all this shit recently...well, you kept coming into my mind, and I couldn't escape it, and it didn't feel good. Figure you would appreciate knowing that.

But you and Ashad would not leave my fucking head and I felt empty inside, and then problems with Jenn just added salt to that wound. I felt like I was as stupid as a thirdrate poormans william hung and it sucked. So, the thing that I couldn't escape from was the ones that told me to fuck off (with the exception of the heartfracturer who doesn't count) were all the people I valued...and who I took for granted. So, what the fuck is wrong with me?

Well, here is what I've come up with, and I cmae up with it after watching High Fidelity late one night gratefully able to watch anything, let alone something that somehow snuck in a little life lesson on me as I was just starting to hate music snobs like them, and then I realized...

I am one. Well not a music snob. And the worst part is...I don't know what kind of one I am...just a basic all purpose snob. I was hating Jack Black so much and so hard and I had to ask myself why. Because I am him....well the character him. I mean I bitch about everything, but with most thing I don't know shit about it. I like to think I'm cool and special but I realize I am nothing but a normal basic bullshit stupid bastard and will be for a long time if not forever, but that I think I have a lot to offer the world, but I just can't seem to stop tripping myself up and stumbling over the stupid stuff. (oh and I'm trying to watch my language again after dropping an Fbomb at my grandmother on the phone, so it will explain why this sounds different if it does) I am still going with the bullshits though since they are just me, but also, they are like the new ass or bitch, ok in most circumstances. So its like the who random rabbi who said once something like you shouldn't claim credit for studying the Talmud because it is your whole purpose for being here. Well that has been slapping me upide the head continually lately.

So I just want to say I'm sorry I'm a dumbass and give you an idea that the shit end of the stick has been stuck up my ass since 'fuckoff simon' has become the OC of the summer with anyone that I feel attached to wanting to get into the action.

I don't know much. But I know you're cool, and I know I didn't realize that soon enough, and I know I miss knowing you.

And I'd probably dick you over again. So don't let have that chance again. At least anytime before we're 30 :) I don't know what to say and I don't know if I send this that you'll even read it…but what I really want to say is something strange and its nice knowing you won't be looking at me as I fumble over it since you don't have to have the torture of daily doses of simon right now, but I feel pity for you come schooldays in that way and so all I know is that I want to say but not really knowing how to say it cause its not something I really know about…but please know and not just from today on, but from the first day I met you and will continue on because I realize how soothing it is to be around you, how rad you are with no apparent cause, that well…well basically your always going to be important to me inside and …. (…if I ever can get it out) :) ………

Becky, I love you

And you know I don't mean that in the corny way or in the fairytale way…I don't know what way it is….but…

Thank you for showing me your heart, and making me realize how beautiful they are and how important they are to make anyone beautiful. Sorry I had to tanish and dent it in the process.

You'll be in my thoughts with every Mirrorball McLachlan song, and in every smile that you see on someone's face that gives you that glimpse of that genuine soft real person shining through from the inside

Simon Stanley

Subj:	**TEB and You**
Date:	Thr. 9/02/2004 10:08:48 PM EST
From:	ssspellman@everydaysanctuary.net
To:	LaLaLevine@everydaysanctuary.net

Tisk tisk LissaAnn – disconnecting number and not telling nobody! Benn so long!!!

So… AhHa! I found you :)

Had to say hi and that there is a reason why…

I'm Blinded…

"I stay right here in the shower, I want to go down on you for an hour"

Just heard this song out of no where for the first time in forever sitting at this place reading this crazy book someone gave me, appreciating all the crazy coincidentals that make us us and all of a sudden you're here with me. It's fucking crazy and I'm happy with it. I'm happy all of you this brings back into my mind and into my pants, but also so, so much into my heart. I know I could straight off say that mind and pants thing and you would understand that, and be okay with it still, and that's what brings the heart into it. I wanted to tell you I appreciate you and all that I am from you. Not bad, huh?
How do you do it?
I don't know, do you? does anyone?

I don't know what else to write. Don't want to go off stupid, but to say you're with me with nearly every TEBing except SemiCharmed Life and Jumper (fucked up intense won't go into it elem sch moments). So…know that Blinded from the Third Eye does exactly that to my concentration because it brings up you.
You do that to my concentration every time you entire it. You inside me from them, as much as that singers inside you when you want him to be especially if you have a poster of him on the cieling.
:)

As much as I want to be inside you someday if I am ever good enough to grow up be able to open up and grow up enough to you and be able to handle it with you. I have no idea what the hell that means, but it seems like you'll understand what I'm talking about because whenever I babble you seem to get it, and that is why I love knowing you, and that is why I'm so happy I have bits of you in me as I go through all this craziness of life now and already know for so many reasons I'm appreciaiting it even before going through it. Crazy! And that's you.

So anxiously awaiting the hope-to-be time when we're both in the same city, for more than 24 hours, and dreaming of a time we may ever have ourselves permanently in the same area code.

1000 Julys to you, and memories of those couple special June days never forgotten and because shared vividly with you.

A friend and always more,
Simon

Subj:	**de simon loco, un email por Jenn, mmmkay?**
Date:	Sun. 9/05/2004 4:05:16 AM EST
From:	ssspellman@everydaysanctuary.net
To:	jennzen@everydaysanctuary.net

I'm going to go with this whole coolness and feeling right thing while it lasts.

I'm sorry I'm such a douche. I'm a tool. I'm a lamely amazingly clumsy fool. I know.
    I'm an asshole. After you said it 20 times I think I finally realize it. And admitted it. Isn't it the first step to recovery? Okay?

So I've been getting all deep and personal lately. And with school starting back up, been feeling pretty solo without my normal crowd since the June but really since last year ended which you could probably tell but which I never really talked about and well well so they really aren't my friends anymore I guess. But I've tried to figure out what it is and why its happening and what's going on with me and so lately I've been reading a lot of funky things and been pretty mellow except in my mind, and well its been weird and I don't know how long it will last so I'm trying to in the most respectable way I can to you what I don't think I ever did before.
    And it all stems from a great night I had that I wasn't able to share with you. And it really dampened my spirit to realize that I wasn't going to be able to tell you.
    I've never been able to say this so well. But...I have nothing to say, I have no idea what is going on...I've gotten off the carousel that wasn't good for me. But in the process I lashed out and hit away all the cool peeps. So I am just going to go class and going to work when school comes round, and hanging out with really cool people when I can if they're willing...(hint hint)...so its all so much less socializing...but it is so much better somehow. So can't really explain all of that, but I can say a lot of about the inside stuff...and so even if we

never are friends again...just know I wasn't being a fool...anymore. Well as much anyway.

    Well I guess this whole selfadmittance, egokicking sort of whatever it is I'm going through stems from the confrontations with so many cool people in my life. My parents were all going BS stupid the other day about school and the importance of picking a college and it just got into the Charlie brown teacher thing of Wah Wah WahhhWah, and they were saying application this and graduation that and it made me realize something...I couldn't imagine all the people I would want at a graduation party getting along...why is that? I'll have to invite this person but that means then those other two can't come with the whole bringing back issues sort of thing.
    But anyway, it all stems from this thing with Tim. Or at least its only through it I can figure my shit out...And I guess I knew all this shit already, but anyway so that hit a head recently and so at least its all out and done with before school starts but so all these personal realizations came in the form of this cool kid from Quincy I met the other weekend. So this kid Sao who I guess was named after some prince or something is so much like Tim, bad ass stater in two sports and seems like tons of friends and flocks of girls and wicked cool...and well he just got back from spending some of the summer traveling around somewhere with friends and I guess what it is, is in him I saw all the potential that Tim has just in a younger shell, but maybe I guess without the shell? Without the whole attitude and ego of Taz...Does that makes sense with the difference? Basically the outside in all the specifics, he is just like Tim....except his eyes are open past the big ass blinders that seems to have helped create such a powerful layer of bullshit called Taz   Basically this kid, who could be just as bad as a Tazattitude I suppose, but the fact is, he was all meeting new people in strange situations and was being all fluid like a real person rather than that projected shit that Tim does (or I've done) when he's not in a totally solo and secure kind of situation. Its sad, so sad, to see Tim turn into Taz in the heartbeat when anyone comes around the corner or whatever. And anyway, so that made me realize some shit about myself.

The fact is, I know I am a good person inside, thank you for what you said about it being there way back when, but yea...what, this past year I've dicked over or been wicked mean to almost everyone I like? And I've dicked them over without even fully realizing it or putting any consideration of them into it. And it was when I was trying to be whatever the fuck the situation needed. The Everclear song, Everything to Everyone? Yea. That was me. Probably don't have to tell you that. So this year, its going to be me leaving school after class for work most days rather than home after practice and Masshole hours like every other semester before and I don't have that whole schedule and social group and autobooked weekends and I am amazed at how empty I feel. And I realize because that was what was filling the space of "me" so easily. And now I don't have that, out of choice, but the pull back ot it is intense, and so I know without working more and all the newer people met and the ones hopefully in school I'd probably be back into it and my Who Am I and WTF self in that Tim-to-Taz instant heartbeat sort of way.. So, yea I'm having a little ball-withdrawal :)

I guess it comes down to the fact that my shit stinks and doesn't stink in a good way, and well, I finally realize I need to stop trying to hide it and pretend it isn't' there. Like playing Elimadate with everybody and their mom but unable to find someone you match with, cause you can't even own up to yourself with yourself so you can't find anyone not certifiably crazy...and then are shocked or something.

But so its like with TimTaz, I have to just accept that in total, it is Tim, and that he has his flaws...and just understand that he is so good inside and has such potential, but that doesn't mean that he actually will follow through. And what I've come to figure out is that he messes it up with the exact thing that I'm using to push him away so I don't feel a loss for losing him as a friend, more I feel a door closing in myself...the same feeling exists there with the closing of him and the soc/lax element. They feel the same which is strange. But that is the feeing I get when I write those rant or bitch about someone, its that feeling of closing doors, and so basically I guess its that I'm closing any chance of knowing the person and so I have to ask myself why am I closing the doors. And I'm sor sorry I was doing that to you. And to anyone...I was just fighting back from Danielle doing it to me, and the fucked up thing was I felt it was good to do it? I don't really know what the fuck this whole same feeling shit is all about, but guess I'll figure that out later. But at this point its just way weird. So yea, needless to say, Ashad really kicked the shit out of my brain today with all this shit. (part of the reason I can't sleep) you can probably guess the other. :)

So it was all coming down to the fact I was putting melodrama over any bit of morality, and then blaming everyone else for the lack of it. And I'm still trying to get past that all putting bullshit over buddies and trying to work through that. For Taz for example, for him, he's putting gayness over goodness, and with you I guess I was putting ego over emotions. I am sorry for that. I wasn't there for you and I'm sorry. But whatever the case may I'm feeling like I must be the squirrelly dude from Amelie who was all staring at the finger that was pointing at the important thing rather than looking at the important thing. And it just sorta comes together with these books Ive been picking up past few weeks. There was a book ashad borrowed out to me that I totally spaced about but started flippin through that like 1000 page book by this in and out Catholic about the history of the Christian churches and the Jews...Constantine's Sword. Yea, ya wonder why my head is a tad messed up...and I haven't even gotten to the serious shit...anyway, so yea already in school mode and haven't even gone to class yet. Anyway, so it hit come from this dude used to be a priest but he got disillusioned or something I guess with between the divine and the dogma when they were saying opposite things. And just that sort of acceptance of personal problem and introduction to whoever is reading it along with this TimTaz shit and all the movies I've been watching lately have put me in a place to realize what it comes down to with me. Ashad outed me (I know) with all my bullshit and all of a sudden I saw it with the right light, that I try to hide all these parts of me fearing they'll get damaged or something. But what I only just was realizing, was that it isn't that they are damaged by anyone you care about as long as they know it's a part of you that isn't negotiable, so if it gets a little dirty, its not going to get damaged. I've been exposing myself to real world people...not Real World people. I know. I know. Fucking amazing isn't it?? I guess Ashad taught me that. He has so many weird contradictory parts of him, but at the same time he makes it allgood somehow, and something Trace said to me recently made me realize why...because he isn't hopping around wondering how to do it, but just makes sure he's pointing the right direction and just does it. And looking back I guess it was showing through it all when the shit hit the fall this summer like not being pissed at Taz and them for being all gaybashing...but at me for not standing up for myself. It sounded so strange when he said it, but it at the same time made just so much sense....but only after the final fuckall with Tim. I finally stopped trying to be accepted by all them and move on with me...and then it was clearer...That they only have problems, I guess we all only have problems with things we don't identify with and whatnot and by me trying to refute or fight them doing what they did I wasn't simply just saying that a part of me was knowing people like that or being whatever I am and get over it or don't but it isn't something negotiable. I was like, "whoa" with that whole sorta epiphany light bulby kinda thing. It was like this, we all are shallow to start with...you can't get pissed off at someone for staying shallow when they don't even know about the rest of the pool and have never had anyone help them into it. Makes sense to me since I'm such a panzy of a swimmer. I never left the sides of a pool and then boom one day some asshole from school all pushes me in and I freak. But it took someone later on to help out to get me comfortable out there. And so, I guess I'm saying, I'm sorry I hit you as I was flailing around wildly as I lost track of the edge of the pool. Ashad has been helping me learn to swim in these metaphorical waters. The best kind of friends do.

    The other kind of best friends are the ones that kick you in the ass or throw tomatoes at you like you're wearing a target when you need it.

So before whatever this is in me goes away I wanted to apologize to you, thank you, and let you know that I care about you, and in the lifelong friend kind of way...I love you.

Thank God, Praise Allah, and all the others that I won't have to see you tomorrow after writing this, its been hard enough dealing just with the thoughts of you lately... But know, as much as we've always been hanging out on opposite wavelengths, you've always been appreciated deep because you still wanted to hang out with me but only when it was the real me that should want to get into progressively deeper waters. I'm only just now understanding that there is that deepness, and understanding that there is that Jennness, and only just now able to tell you that I know that. Its one of those you knew but you didn't know you knew? You know? (and you should know that "Jennness" is in my computer dictionary now because it is a proper word and term) :)

In so many ways what I miss most with you is all the stupid shit that we were with those stupid hissyfits of ours because you've been cool enough to not let me get away with shit that I need to be called on or hopefully vice versa can come some day, when I get a backbone, say? :) I can't imagine enjoying life as much if you weren't in it. Sorry I put ego above the education with you.

We give each other shit for some of the stupidest things. And there is some grooviness in that as you might say. I laugh at you for being some sort of wannabe hippie soy freaky, and you wouldn't let me get away with being a Mr Smith-like clone of the establishment or whatever you said...but we came from the same little pool. I even showed you my little weener once ;) And from those younger years, you've been important to me, even if I never said it or showed it or knew it.

Thank you.

I hope this shit never happens again, I guess though you're entitled to one...I could be the one to tell you to go to hell this time. "You go to hell, you go to hell and you die Kyle" God we better never hate each other forever, cause then South Park and so much more will be ruined for both of us right? And we can't have that, now can we?

I finally found that compelling reason for us to makeup. Good job Simon.

(The good Simon) :)

You're cool – makeshift sis,
and you're very missed,

Simon Stanley

Antiblog de simon

9-6-04 1:08am

    Yea, um...of course all the shit comes up right afterwards...life saying, oh you think so huh? Like the sequal to the be careful what you wish for, the put up or shut up you little bitch. The fucking annoying rotated show that comes on after Friends. I'm all feeling big and bad with all the cool big brain books I've been checking out and then that bookcrossing shit comes confrontin again in the middle of my week of halfway healthy public egodeflating.

    So with schools starting up soon, I feel like I'm already full with enough syllubusi or whatever....so I have all my selfhelp going on upon a litcourse selfstumbledupon.. so.....Who's got a fullboat of selfassigned silly-bis??...who kicks ass? I do ☺

    Yea...so it goes: thought I was all badass, hanging out there with that Britiamerican Painey and David and Augusten and Tom and getting it all and dismissing Painey for being short and shit and wishing I had more of a challege like the shit the other guys have for stories that happen to them as if scripted Shakespeare comedy or soemthing....so enter life with a bitchslap...Me Get Skooled One Day

    So it becomes....who's about to get his ass kicked by some old Russian guy? ☺
    .....I am.....

    But I at least kicked my own ass first before this Fyodor fucker gets a chance. In the past four days I was able to pull my pants down and flog myself egoly with Lissa and Jenn and in person with Ashad which was ubberintense. Bet he would enjoy that comparison with flogging... Don't know what will come from the insinde open boarder policys but it sure feels good and I'm sure they won't piss on me...except ot take the piss. ☺

So anway I trained it out to Davis yesterday, (Sat) after Ashad shockingly emailed me, he was all willing to give us a shot as friends again which was super cool and if anything he said he had some pics from 5/17 and wanted to give me copies since it was such a mem day and shit...which was right on time as Taz was all back into shittalking trash mode which I'm done with cause its like he's on the rag, but three weeks on, only one week off, and I was all waffling on the whole Just Say No factor towards all that shit so perfect timing helping me with my final FUCK YOU and CYA. Imean as much as I want to play just feels so fake and so...what...stale? Tired? Spend hours a day in order to ride the bench and trashtalk myself each time the convo goes bigot mode? No thanks.

    Anyway, so All of a sudden I'm able to be around Ashad again for a coffee and a chat and we just had a great time, the convo just fucking took off, I found myself apologizing and not feeling too awkward about it. And he ends up apologing too!! It was crazy, he was all talking about being a hypocrite, dissing me the way he did being no better than anything he'd always hated others doing to him and shit so he just wanted to wipe things clean whit me and let it go where it may or something like that is how he said it. guess it all came to a head with him when his family all got a call from Tehran (sp) I think that his dad's dad died...and he felt all sorts of shit since he never approved of them being here in the US and certainly didn't know about Ashad being gay but he knew that he didn't like homosexuals, which is why they didn't tell him, but that near the end he said to tell them the sons in the UK and US and families that he wasn't angry with then, just missed them, and shit like that. And so I guess Ashad got an eyeopening sorta thing from that. But anyway, it was crazycool because he was all unsure about things with this next semester in Amherst because he's signing up for a study abroad for spring but didn't' know if it'd go through so what classes this semester in case and shit like that which is all dependent on all that legal shit taken care of to go to Iran for some sort of cross cultural research project and had been worried about the whole family reaction and stuff to who he was if they found out and stuff but that the bittersweet of it was that now more than ever he wanted to go but was so guilty that it was after his gfather died that he felt like that.. Talk about intense...and fuck, like I said, he is a prized piece...nothing like being involved in five or ten camps that all have bones to pick and at worst what told me to fuck off for a few weeks...pretty on par it seems like. Anyway hope he gets it though. He definitely is one special person.

And anyway, so he helped me feel good about my decision to try and change up and just work and study more. It was an amazing time. and then all of a sudden its fucking sunsetting and we barely realized it being in the back of the place instead of at the sidewalk tables. So it was all really great.

And so on top of it all, before Ashad got there and the book guy, there was a lesbian group or something sitting around the couches all chatting about this and that, and it was so strange to just sit there and just be reading surrounded by them all coffeetalking and have them just go on as normal, funny, I was able to read and concentrate and occasionally hear the funny tibits they were talking about without much worry. Is it weird that I can work better like that than in a library or at school? Anyway and then one chick said something just so perfectly wickedly awesomely funny. They all got into their stories of coming out to their parents and shit, and this one lady was all talking about how her parents were relieved to know and shit but that they were just happy that she was and was able to tell them...cause apparently she was one of like 8 or 9 kids and then they bust out with the, "finally! One of ours is! We were wondering if that would ever happen, figured the odds were good" and she goes all careful what you wish for and said she was all letdown somehow in some small way for being let down afte antcipiating some mild drama. Fuckig hilarious, they all cracking up living through her ease of Out!! Too bad more people can't be like that though. Be cool to see the rest of Ashad's fam be cool like his rents were bout it....seriously, show up at the big ol whatever gathering they have be like showing up with an Islamic boyfriend. "Ashad! we're so happy that you've come come with a nice person, and to top it off he's a Sunni boy, how nice. Not necessary, but way to go!" We can only hope. Just happy my parents don't play the fucking conditional love shit with the Jewish gf card like so many others. So fucking wrong. What the fucks the point of carrying on the legacy or whatever if it doesn't include you. Hollow and empty is what itd be at that point. I like the shit Tracy was telling me though how you can make it what you want. Since you are technically by name, that Jewish holidays are your holidays…but you can still go out and not limit your dating options. Best of both worlds. Ashad gets a few breaks a day to pray if he wants to use them. Maybe I can do both ☺

    So the book thing. So what was all what I got into as I trained home, and as fucked up as it was, reading ten pages of it then hooked me for the rest, but the rest being about a thousand pages! So some fucker as I got there early and was waitng for Ashad on the couches in the back all is scoping out the room and so I look up from my book and am eyebrow raising him with the WTF look as he is checking out everybody in there in that creapy sort of way and then he just comes over to the table I hope to just grab the Globe or Windows that were on the crazy nutsnbolts table but no, he drops a book and then all just straight up walks out and disappears while looking over his back the whole time. I scope him the whole time he leaves and only hten sit up to check it out, and low and behold another one of those little BCtags. Quite cool. But yea that, ah shit factor. ASF…or OSF? It's a 1000 page doesevsky book. The brothers Karamazov or something that ive never heard of but having heard that guys cool shit with stories. Um…I do enjoy the fact that I now have a fucking Russlit book to go through for free if I want in total secret and and no timelimit and pressure from being graded at it. But in some ways it feels like an assignment, like the sketchy cool dude picked me out for some of this ancient torture, hmmm, you look too comfy there laid back and legs crossed with your little Sedaris book of stories (god I probably looked just a little gay but oh well), so fuck you, I command you to read this! I mean seriously, you can be half way through and still have a couple months to go?!? And its fucking slow reading, fucking thick lined heavyass story. Like its some sort of dare because how dare you think you're a cool tool from reading something with more staying power than a SouthBeach shit, so here, you are chained now to something having thinkness riviling whatever the either of the trios ClancyChritonGrisham or RobbinsBurroughsSedaris wrote this year and I know you won't not get through it even two years later cause youown't let your ego be able to know you got licked by a book. Hahahah. But at least I don't have to go through a fucking lecture of background and stopping every other paragraph to analyze it to the point of death of enjoyment like in school, that would be the torture from the looks of it in those back page notes which have just enough. There's a reason to be happy not being a Russian Jew with the languagelearning curce and shit, don't know how theyall did it. The fucked up part thou was how the back sounded appealing...like a modernday scene of drama and personality set in the past like it was on Broadway but that is stay-tuneable like a television series without the soap opera melodrama like how the OC was at the start. Fuckkng thing starts out like a movie preview ... some asshole dude killed and his son imprisoned for it but no ones really knows whathappened cause everyone hated him but there are three brothers from different woman all with bones to pick and one is trying to be a monk while the others are dirty playas or thieves and shit but with all the astriocratic bullshit but with the social commentary microscope like something inbetween Shakespeare and Vonnegut, who speaking of which I really need to pick up more of with school coming up for the regular installment of somewhatsanity semester comic relief, that is of course unless we succeed with the third species attempt to commit suicide...god I'm such a little reference snob, my antiblogging turning into some fucking rap song of exploits as if there is an audience for it I'm speaing to or being all Taz preachy jesus namedropping shameless pluger. Look, I gotta wristband WWKS What would Kurt say bout it?

    Godamnit, its official. my antiblogging has become a blog.

    That means I have to either delete them all, like the bimonthly purging of porn so I can keep my concept of selfrespect normalcy and stable harddrive...or I just have to bite the fucking bullet and say I was wrong. (Ego: No!!!! delete delete delete!!!!!). funny thou there is so much egoing going on acting like I'm all badass when I'm just stpid shit that happenes to find a lot of fucking rad crazy people to sponge off of. Suppose at least I'm not using them... I'm such a flirty little social passive sponge. OMG (and I'm so over the overly ABBR thing)...well the stupidshit ones. Eddie Izzard could be my mentor. Eddie's cool with his I'm smart but I'll all act like I don't know what I'm talking about and then just drop in these couple little tidbits that tell you I know it all sort of in the year blablablabal...then... Nooo...its cold! its cold! Suppsoe there are worse things to be than an espresso addict dramaqueen.

Ok. That was fucking fluid as all hell.

Hi. My name is Simon, and I'm a caffeinated dramaqueen.

But what I really need to put into check is this shit shit, along with the fucking Fbombs. But, might as well go with it in this ABentry, so where was I...must admit I'm glad I was able to neg. punishment with the rents. Trading TV and working weekend nights from the pike shit...dude, I pretty much got away with that shit ☺ with all the books lately it pretty much an even trade, still getting my storytime , but then to be able to get out of fucking lame ass Wallyworld as long as there is an Ashad or Trace as the reason?...super chill. Who knows, commuting to BH from home might be able to work next year with this sorta setup. Although UMassAm could be just far enough away to keep things cool and copasetic. What movie is that fucking word from? OK that's gonna piss me off   Anyway...so oh yea Vonneguted WWIII...you know what they say, third times a charm. WWIII baby, the tension and expectations have been building...from the producers that brought some of the Iran-Contra and Gulf Wars, directed by the worldwide resource managers responsible for hallaburton, comes a feature bound to dazzle your senses and take your breath away. Literally. And skin too. Staring the anti-Christ (but which side is he on??? we'll keep you guessing until the very end!!), and introducing the new Russian mob complex in association with near East Asian upcoming players. Dude they could hype this more than all the StarWars! And its got the whole apocalyptic tie-in. So after Mel got everyone all salivating with sacrelig and the mother of all "oops! Our bad, sorry Messiah..." it's a perfect time...as long as it isn't a Mel or Bruce shootemup maincharacter and they refrain from focus on New York blow up yet again. God I really have no attention span, but that fucking guy's gotta go, but at leats I can always track back to whatver it was, just see, I'll do it, right after I go verbal bitchslap upside NYs head...the city's already lost and f-ed up enough, what is blowing it up going to do? You'll only give everyone up enough to have insurance a big check and have some clean slate. Don't give them that helping hand. A place that is so fucking crazy and the people that are "successful" fucking jailcelled on that beadbought island prison. I mean I can't wait to get out of Waltham, but I sure as hell am not going to replace it with an even worse example that thinks it's the greatest city in the world. If that's true, what does that say about the rest of the world? God. That is a fucking sad thought. But seriously, that is getting old all the NY destructions, especially htat one fucking twat that does it three or four times in his movies, give us a little credit, our memory recalls do go back a couple years still. Well some of us. Maybe NY is like the schoolbully you were always told will go away if you just ignore it. Lets try that!! Probably wont work though since they are so fucking irriating there they will just keep climbing in your face the second you have anything else occupying your mind like a three year old attention hog but that whores themselves for biweekly paychecks for their prada or Armani. Had to take that swing at fashion while I had the chance... But seriously there are so many other cities to go with, and with memorable skylines and shit to play with. Boston doesn't have to be one of them, but a few short clips could be fun. Inside clip of a packed house at Fenway, Sox/Cubs in the Series and then pan to the Green Monster torn down by a wall of holy fire...great subplot showing neither dreamteam getting a ring since hell didn't freeze over but was instead unleashed on the world by lawyers and businessmen and Yankee fans and Bushes, or Harvard kids and profs running away from locusts or something could work really well on one of those pretty charles riv bridges with maybe a jitterydizzy Radiohead song subtly soundtracked up in the background, good contrast. Dude, how bout god go all 21ts century right before...all of a sudden a website setup like Bruce Almighty-style automatically everyones homepage, with the list of who will be smited that day. Posted at sunrise, for dusk smitings...God giving everyone a day to get things in order and do as they wish with one final sunset as the cherry on top and a chance to finally get all those cherries popped...then, Poof! Yea I can act all smart and shit like I know what the fuck I'm talking a bout when I want to. So where was I... fuck, ok, scroll up and... yes!

    Ok, so the Karamazov stuff will be done. Nearly unianamous decision...Pussysimon all punked out so abstained from voting. I might take me the rest of the year, but a fun thick project to contain my imagination that otherwise would want to be going back to balls and sticks. I'm soooo fucking over balls and sticks. ☺   And this way my ego is happy cause I can act all high and mighty. Oh, I'm sorry I didn't do that fucking pointless bullshit assignment, I was reading some motherlaod RussianLit novel...exec decis, sorry.

    But yea I really need to chill the fuck out with the abbr and whole fuck usage-ing. I don't really give a shit of other peoples opinions are about it but just in that crazy bean can sort of way seems like it really could be watering down whatever I say and makes me crutch onto my surface feelings without knowing what is undernearth like all the awaymessage dependent people are and we won't even get into myspacespacecadets and as I'm afraid to do a CLT-Fing and figure out how many times in this anti-blog blog it was used and I'm already sliding into blogging and better stop before I end up TyPiNg AlL ReTaRdEd and shit, but that's their cup of tea if they LiKe It ThAt Way Koool...but its about time I actually decide on my own something kind of cup or tea or something...I think I'll go with ooooooolong and say oooooo-righttttt and be all chill with the the whole storytimeDQSimon sorta thing and actually stick to the fucker. The thing. Stick to the thing that I decided. Follow through on the decision to better articulate my thoughts and self. Ok? Motion carried.

    So on this fucking day, I am committing to decrease my fucking fuck fucks.

You're fucking mission if you choose to fucking accept it...
What a fucking challenge.
What a fucking anti....blog

Oy vey pretty much sums it up.

Antiblog de simon

9-7-04 1:45am

Ummmm...
Damn deep...

"a longing to love instinctively from the depths of one's being - you put that beautifully, and I'm so happy you have such an urge to live. I think that everybody should, above all else on this earth, love life."
"Love life rather than the meaning of it?"
Certainly, it must come before logic, as you said, must certainly come before logic, for only then can one come to understand the meaning. I've thought that for a long time already. You're halfway there, Ivan, half your task is accomplished. You love life."

Fyodor Dostoevsky's Karamazov Brothers, page 89 Alyosha and Ivan

Damn Deep...

Antiblog de simon

9-7-04 3:28pm

Who the fuck does that Miller twittwat think he is? Go into his office to switch a class and I have to get "counseled." Change a class? Get 20 questions. Then get chasised? In the first fucking week?!?! Shit. At all?! Don't you have anything better to do? I felt like I was Cartman at the Fucking optometrist...I just wanted to change my schedule you fucking asshole! MY! Schedule!!!! And you Fucking comparing me to fucking Holden Calfield? Who the fuck are you?? I don't give a fuck whats wrong in your life that you can't figure it out so you have to tell me where I should focus my efforts god damn it you are out there trying to telling me and wtf 14 year old girls how they should live there lives because you can't figure your shit out after 50 years, fuck you. I'll be damned if you're allowed to 'counsel' my sister come the time. I was all going to work on my poor language, but not right now, this is a fucking rant, this is a fucking a fucking cool Mr Miller of the Dennis persaution sort of rant. Richard Miller asshole. Dick Miller you fucking asshole, you are the peak and end off of asshole...get smacked by a bus right in front of me? I'll sport one of those stealthy grins as I walk on by looking up at the sky and beaming a bit brighter. Speaking of 14 year old girls....you are the type of guy that dates girls in high school even when like way into college aren you, cause they are the only ones left that will look at you so adoringly thinking you are just such cool shit when in fact you aren't even good enough to be a scummy asshole of a guy but the self-deprecating...yea see I know words like that and I know what they mean and I know what the FUCK Holden Calfield was all about...kind of guy so you go find people that don't know any better so you can fucking starting a koolaid cult and have to rotate admireres though because they eventually wise up but for now they won't actually know the difference between minor leaguers and the big leaguers so you're set. You are the washout guy that plays a half a season in the majors and can't cut it but you go back to coach little league with all your "wisdom" of being a "major leaguer" because you will call yourself that so you can hear those little sweaky voiced 'ooos' but it will only work if you do way young little league, anyone over age 12 will see through your bullshit cause they are starting to work on contructing their own. Get em before they got them egos!! So you can't get anything good going on in your lfie, your life is totallyl without inner bling...so you sport the material sort in cars and stories of where you've gone and what you've read, riiight...and since no one has ever really dealt with your shit besides whoever was stupid enough to marry you feel the the pathetic little man you are and run behind all the smoke and mirrors so no one will see. Except we all can tell you fucking twat! And so what do you do? You be come a school counselour. You're a fucking school counselor! You didn't become a fucking preacher. So quit acting like your one and an expert on life and getting to the promised land. You try to guide my life, help me get through my 'struggles of adolescence'??? FUCK YOU! YOU NEVER LEFT YOURS!!!!!!!!!!!!!!!!!

How they fuck you do you think you can tell me what to do with mine?? Fucking hell. Keep your shit locked up. I don't give a fuck   I know that's what you were trying to do you goddman asshole! Trying to "help" me with suggestions that could 'open doors and shed some light'? And then you strageicly drop in catcher in the rye convienently in between the others?   Going all pretneious and saying you not there to critizicsce or judge but to help and that all those stories just may be interesting to read some day but then but then basically saying I should relate and understand a character like Calfield because he is a 'benchmark character of American literature'?   Whose review did you steal? And you would be the one to judge me though if I plagerized, riiight Oh and I heard how you said it too. See funny thing about voices, you can say one thing and mean another. Did you know that? Did you know that there is a great big hole in your curtain? So you think I am a loser and have no idea who I am of what is going on in the world and have a giant chip on my shoulder and think I'm just so perfect and end up running awayfromt whatever is outside my messed up little head cause I'm scared? And then you look at me with those eyes like I'm a helpless little dog that peed on the carpet? Riiight...and then trying to go all arrogant indigent teacher mentor bullshit and try to explain to me the moral of the story. Yeaa...drop it in the middle of the list and say its just "food for thought" and then start going on in detail about it? SOOOO smooth...stupid hsit.   Excuse me? I KNOW THE FUCKING STORY. IT MAKES TOO MUCH FUCKING SENSE TO ME YOU HAVE NO IDEA. And I think about it, and I think about my own Holdenness a lot, but there is just this teeny weeny little detail that keeps floating up.... I ACTUALLY KNOW I'm FUCKING MESSED UP ALREADY AND FUCK THINGS UP A LOT WHEN I KNOW BETTER BUT CAN"T HELP BUT FUCKING UP SOMETIMES CAUSE I ALWAYS AM FUCKING CLUELESS ABOUT SOMETHING OR ANOTH?EIR BECAUSE I'm FUCKING HUMAN !!!!. But funny thing is I really don't want to announce it all the time show it and admit it all the time to other people in public. My bad. Thanks for putting a spotlight on it. Cheers. you asshole

 and you know what while we're at it, lets see here, what have we got? You're totally a socialinept, coulnd't place your image into any term because ytour a fucking mismatch of manican templates because its all store windowbought in Natick, have the wife and 2.3 kid perfect world that you adertise like you took out a billboard ad with clear channel but can only be contenet with that with a pack of smokes and a lot of coffee and only go home when you have to and prolly booze onec there and for a job you have to have total authority over something to make up for being a total fcking retard with life so you have to get youself some letters after your name so you can downtalk teenagers and force them to call you "Dr" in order ot feel secure morewith yourself as you go on telling them in poor mans woody allen character manipulative ways that they are off the right track but you have the right map and in that, its all about me but its all your fault or respondsibioltiy but I know everything and whats best in whatever sigtutaion kind of way you take up the to "help" thinking to yourself that youst be some sort of divine fucking manifestation of manifest desinty here just for others that are lost so you can feel purpose when really you aren't shit but want to make it seems like you are model citizen of normal and whats in demand and then assult people with this I'm so smart or wellread or cultured in your face to prove it to you I'm not weakn and stupid but really I'm trying to convince myself but I really have nothing to offer anyone so

I'll just try to make everyone feel shittier so I can squeeze myself by rather than doing anything remotely challenging that could require learning new things and gettinb betterwith anything that isn't on the NY times bestseller list to try to "keep up with things" but oh no it takes a chance of unknown and failure so I can't do it cause I have as scared as a five year old girl in a horror movie but wait I have this cheap tie and shirt on so I can look like I have my shit togetherbut really I'm just some stupid sad bottom feeding opporetunist who would always take the last appitzier when someone gest up to the bathroom and distracts everyone else and then shortchange the server on the tip after asking them for eight thousand considerations and demands in that I'm special and deserve concern and your time and care but I won't even genuinely say thank you because I'm a fucking inbred purebred dog sort of lame twat.

You are a waste of oxygen and a perfectly unappreciated SUV, I pity your kids from the moment you open your mouth and I hope they become exacty what you hate/ Not out of spite, but because they see the bullshit that you are in all incarnate and decide to check out everything you aren't and realize its all cool shit and then you get to go through the rest of life getting even more indigent and can find solice with ten or twenty cats after you're wife goes off and fucks the first person that has anything remotely interesting to say and does the Lays potatochip shit after one bite and never goes back. I hope your wife fucks a woman and realized no dick is better than your dick And now my mind is on your dick...and this is fucked up...so I'll put it back onto your shaking shivery scared little ego that you protect by insulting others. Ooo, saw through that one. CauseI'm working my way away...see howt hat works?

You try to ehlp me in life? I don't need your help...at least I'm trying to live life now, even as bullshit as it feels at times especially when having to be around someone like you. But at least I'm trying to love it...and be half way there. But you mourn life. How fucking sadare you. You just want us to all wear black to mourn your inability to cope. How selfish and lame are you

And you want me to come back in next week after 'settling in and cooling down'? ...you going to go Frued and analyze my fucking dreams then? I have a lot of dreams about fucking does that mean I am obsessed with it? Will you tell me thats bad because you haven't gotten any even with a wife for most of this millennium?

Asshole

Goddamn fucking lame ass asshole fucking pissant asshole hole hole hole hole....god what a buzz kill, now I gotta get ot work .... Asshole, beyond a reasonable doubt asshole

...and I'm spent.

Ahhhhhhhhhhhh, so that's how Jenn felt I bet in that email...interesting. had to get all that out now. Maybe I'll save this for graduation time. a little postgrad fuck you

Heres to not quitting heres to going all the way, yay

Back to afew pages of some 19th Cen Russians before heading out for some 21st coffee roastin work

Antiblog de simon

9-8-04 12:45pm @ lunch

    With school starting and trying to better be me, I'm going to go into these ABs and going cleancut as much as I can, only have the redlines under the things that should be there. Like all the shit that needs to be said and is right on but isn't honored by Webster as being proper. Supercool. Badass. Just like Jennness...Not redlined anymore. Here we go, Baby!

    But as all this semester of shit gets started I'm realizing how much I miss the feeling from back in the day, when things were simple and like when you could be watching Scooby Doo and actually being anxious and in suspense, wondering who the bad guy would turn out to be. And of going over to family holiday times and not caring how you were dressed and dreading talking to people. When all you had to answer was what grade you were in and was it fun and you just said whatever it was and yes it was and then you could go eat and play and not care knowing they'd ask you again six months later. Back when it seemed like you understood everyone, when you weren't being judged by family, friends were friends even if they were in the same school or not, and no one was townie, redneck, homie, hippie or otherwise.

    Wait a minute, townie, redneck and hippie are proper English but not homie? How dare you Microsoft, I'll put a stop to that...or a start to it.

    There.

    So, we're not living in a Simon AB world where homie is any less genuine as townie or supercool or snog can feel comfy with comfortable and just plain cool. I'm back in charge of my language, like being back in the groove with the Scooby or the sketchy friends before they were sketchy.

    Now I'm feeling like I'm back in the day. Today.

Back in the day

Subj:	**Dave IM 9-9**
Date:	Thr. 9/09/2004 7:41:25 PM EST
From:	ssspellman@everydaysanctuary.net
To:	ssspellman@everydaysanctuary.net

EQPhreak: WHATS UP?
EQPhreak: SO YOU FIND OUT IF YOUR GONNA BE ABLE TO MEET US OUT TOMORROW?
castaspell: yea gotta work,
castaspell: but I should get off early enough though, def want to.
EQPhreak: AH THAT SUX U GOTTA WORK...
castaspell: yea no doubt, its all good though
castaspell: don't know about you but I'm really digging my schedule this year
EQPhreak: NAH, SAME HERE...ENJOYING THE NEW PEOPLE MEETING AND THE INDEP STUDY OPTION FOR ALL US USHist SECOND TIMERS.
Castaspell: yea fucking cool we only haveta be in class the lec days.
EQPhreak: HEY THOU I SHOULD TELL YOU THOU. MY FRIEND JEN KINDA LIKES YOU. THINKS YOUR CUTE
EQPhreak: (HER WORDS)
castaspell: really?? Jen who?
EQPhreak: JEN DELANEY, I KNOW SHES IN THE SAME ROOM RIGHT AFTER YOUR MATH CLASS.. HAS SEEN YOU A COUPEL TIMES AND AFTER SEEING US TALKING THE OTHER DAY WHEN YOU MET JULIE SO SHE ASKED ME ABOUT YOU.
EQPhreak: SO I JUST QUOTED HER WITH THE CUTE THING TO GET THINGS MOVING SINCE I KNO SHE WOULD PUNK OUT.
castaspell: right on, thanks dave. that's cool!
EQPhreak: NO PROB
EQPhreak: SHES REALLY COOL THOU SO DON'T ALL GO FOR HER IF YOUR JUST LOOKING FOR A HOOKUP OR SCAM, COOL?
castaspell: oh yea, def...
castaspell: finally past that
castaspell: you just about refer my past few mnths of bs
EQPhreak: GOOD TO HEAR...AND GOOD LUCK WITH THAT LITTLE FYI

EQPhreak: HEY I GOTTA GO GET DINNER STARTED FOR MY LITTLE SIS
EQPhreak: BUT GIVE ME A CALL AFTER 9 IF YOU WANT TO FIND OUT MORE BOUT HER COOL?
castaspell: cool. way cool :) whats your # again?
EQPhreak: YEA I THOUGHT SO :)
EQPhreak: 617-XXX-XXXX
EQPhreak: SHE MIGHT BE COMIN FRI TOO
EQPhreak: OH AND REMIND ME TO TELL YOU ABOUT THE HALO TOURNEY NEXT WEEKEND
castaspell: cool, thanks. oh yea? def
EQPhreak: SO, I'M FEELING A BIT COOLER NOW, NOW THAT I'M ALREADY SAVEWORTHY.
castaspell: what?
EQPhreak: YOU KNOW...
EQPhreak: ANYTIME WITH A GOOD IM, SOMEONE GIVES YOU A PHONE NUMBER OR THE CONVO GOES WITH SEX OR FLIRTING OR GIRLS THE SHITS SAVED RIGHT?
castaspell: LOL. You fucking called it...was bout to CLT ACV it...
EQPhreak: AH, THOUGHT SO... SO I SCORED MY FIRST SIMON SAVE TONIGHT.
EQPhreak: I COULD ALWAYS GO FOR THE HATRICK AND TELL YOU JEN IS PRETTY DAMN SEXY AND ISN'T VERY SHY ONCE YOU GET TO KNOW HER.
castaspell: no doubt?? cool!
EQPhreak: YEA NO DOUBT
EQPhreak: I SHOULD KNOW. I'M ONE OF HER "BROTHERS" NOW
castaspell: Oh!! You've gotten yourself BROlabeled to? damnnn
EQPhreak: BEST OF BOTH WORLDS THOU...DATEABLE, FRIENDABLE, AND FUTUREABLE
castaspell: yeaa ... true, been tryin to learnthat one
EQPhreak: YEA JUST DON'T GET STUCK INTO ONLY ONE CATEGORY AND YOUR ALL SET
castaspell: good challenge
EQPhreak: DEF
EQPhreak: WELL I'LL LEAVE YOU WITH THAT...THOUGHTS OF COOL AS SHIT GIRL JEN...SHORT, CURVED OUT POWERHOUSE BRUNETE THAT SHE IS
EQPhreak: TTY RIGHT AFTER 9
castaspell: niceeeee :-P
castaspell: peace

Subj:	**makeshift antiblog**
Date:	Sat. 9/11/2004 12:46:13 PM EST
From:	ssspellman@everydaysanctuary.net
To:	ssspellman@everydaysanctuary.net

I was like ten different people last night. And they all felt like me.
I was friendly with school people inside the party
I was a bad ass speedy worker before
I was Sean's old friend from back in the day
I was a cel-pic taking fool throughout with someone's phone
I was an weird little energetic dancer
I was a friendly to Sean's friends who didn't know anyone
I was a chatty flirty funny want to snog but don't want to mess things up with Dave's friend Jen
I was a talkative but smart slightly drunk fool with the couple college people partiers
I was more open with Kristi P, I hope enough to quell problems

The biggest thing though, and happy it didn't get ugly or messy was eye-opening. Basically I put myself into a really piss-poor position, on the receiving end from a really forward girl, and getting flirty and open with someone I wanted to go forward with all before I realized Dave and Company were there...but they weren't the same person and while neither brought bad drama I felt it could have been and then boom...,
I realized for myself, viewing myself I guess, from the outside or something that I need e to change it up and so I chose to deny the lust drug that was accessible from that friend of Tony's and could have come from that chick Erin who I was totally into and stayed clear of the scamming simon.. Don't know how that worked, but I somehow kept all the simons on a track that feels more in the right direction and ended up getting Jen's info after we were all hanging out and. And the fucked up part was, it all stayed quiet and civil and it wasn't to relieve a fight or guilt, but because I actually didn't want to hurt Kristi or Jen or lead on Erin or that other girl. Woah. I still don't want Kristi anymore like last year and want to try things out with Jen but at least Kristi didn't have to witness all that facts first hand in the messed up ways that could have been. Needless to say,

I'm not going to go for any more girls named Kristi for a long time…Hopefully. Friend Jen with one N here I come. :)

makeshift antiblog makeshift sanity, even without sobriety

Antiblog de simon

9-12-04 2:15am

Fucking hell...Fucking deep. Trying to punch through with as much of these Karamazovs before the first real book assignment for class rears its knappyass head. Cause this is just fucking beautiful.

"Love one another my brothers. Love God's people. Jus because we have shut ourselves within these walls, it does not make we any holier than the laity; on the contrary, anyone who has come here has by that very act acknowledged to himself that he is worse than any lay person and all the more deeply he will realize this. If this were not the case, there would be no need for him to come here at all. When however he realizes that not only is he worse than every layman but that he is guilty before all, for everything and before everyone, for the sins of all men, individually as well as collectively only then will he goal of our salvation by attained. For know you this, my dearly beloved brethren each one of us is unquestionably answerable for all men and all things on earth, not only by virtue of the collective guilt of the world, but also individually, for all men and everyone on earth. This realization is the crowning glory not only of the monastic way of life but of every human being on hearth. For monks are just like other people except that they are as all men on earth ought to be. It is only through this realization that our hearts will be moved to boundless, universal, all-consuming love. Thus will each one of us be able to redeem the world and with his tears wash away its sins...Each should attend to his own heart, each should ceaselessly render account unto himself. As long as you are repentant do not be alarmed at your own sin even in the full knowledge of it, and do not attempt to strike bargains with God. Again, I say unto you, - Be humble. Be humble with the weak, be humble with the mighty. Bear no ill will against those who reject, defame, malign, and slander you. Bear no ill will against atheists, false prophets, materialists, even the evil ones, for there are many good ones among them too, especially in our time. Remember them in your prayer: save, O Lord, all those who have no one to pray for them, save also those who do not want to pray to You. And add forthwith: it is not out of pride that I beseech you, for I myself am the vilest of the vile. Love God's people, do not let strangers take possession of your flock, for if you are indolent and full of false pride – or worse still, - avaricious – they will come from all corners of the earth and lure your flock away."

Deep ol fucker.
...
...
...
...
Added 9-14-04 12:15AM

"As to every man being guilty for everyone and everything, quite apart from his own sins," he continued, "you did indeed judge correctly and it is surprising how you managed to get so completely to the heart of the matter straight away ... For everyone has disassociated himself from everyone else in our age, everyone has disappeared into his own burrow distanced himself from the next man, hidden himself and his possessions the result being that he has abandoned people and as in his torn been abandoned. He piles up riches in solitude and thinks, 'how powerful I am now, and how secure,' and it never occurs to the poor devil that the more he accumulates the further he sinks into suicidal impotence... But it is certain that this terrible isolation will come to an end, and everyone will realize at a stroke how unnatural it is for one man to cut himself off from another ... But nevertheless, until then man should hold the banner aloft and should from time to time, quite alone if necessary, set an example and rescue his soul from isolation in order to champion the band of fraternal love, though he be taken for a holyfool. And he should do this in order that the great Idea should not die..."   kicking butt in and kickin it with Super Z Staret in FD's K-doggs p. 379

And articulating my thoughts with the proper expression:

Fucking-A...

<file listed as created and saved on
September 12, 2004 at 8:40 pm>
      -- GG

To whom it may concern,

    I am interested in furthering my education through your school in order to further explore and learn communication and psychology skills and theory so that I may be able to establish a career for myself in a field of media that allows me to reach others with the skills I hope to develop. Because of several factors in my past I became largely fascinated in television and movies, and more recently realized my attraction to books.
    From these interests that I'm only recently aware of I hope to study and work in the fields that will help bring out the skills of storytelling in myself so that I may be able to expose and express my developing worldview to others.

AHHH!!!!!!! This fucking blows!!

Okay, deep breath Simon...
Waa wa wa wa waaa

Screw it, peace out UMASS PS BS til later ...

Antiblog de simon

9-12-04 9:35pm

"Everyman, seen distinctly enough is abnormal, for the normal is only a name for the undifferentiated, for a failure to see the inescapable nuance." Edwin Muir, deemed googible cause of the cool quote, whoever he is

    Ok...shit, I won't complain about my bullshit now comparative to the teenage angst that dude must've had....damnnn.
    Ok, so far I'm digging my teachers this year...scary. It seems with acouple of them that there cool with you as long as you are cool with them,if you're willing to come into class bringing your A-Game. Yea I think I'll do that. Hopefully while A-Rod ends up failing his final in his big ol NYclassroom now that the leaves start turning and I'll bust out with some A-Sim and learn some good shit and go watch the A-Sox bring it. But anyway, digging it.
    You know, throughout journalydiary sort of things I've always gotten way too out of proportioned about girls fancied or obsessed over which explains the deletion frequency. Shit I'm going to wear out that key pretty soon.. and me thinks Ashad be rubbing off on me a bit much with the lingo ey? But suppose at least not rubbing off the wrong way, hey? But yea so a small part of me is selfconscious of it all with the girlys, because the rest of me knows that the amount of worry and concentration on it is so messed up and out of wack...but then somewhere says that its okay as long as it isn't forever and just get over it slowly. And its funny how strangely non--obsessed over Jen I am with knowing whats possible?   Lil' bit freak-ayeeee...
    But the messed up shit is like what Alyosha struggles with I think, he's trying to find himself without any good reference point. Guess I should be happy I have like five or six or whatever. Wonder if I'd be able to navigate without any markers. His family is so gone and messed up so he runs to a monestary. He only can identify himself with what he isn't, a fucking nut like his dad etc, but somehow he doesn't stick to

it. So that brings up a pesky question. What about the people that don't have themselves a Starets? Where is my staret? Ashad fits the bill in so many ways. Jenn and Tracey a lot lately too. And coulpe other over the years could be too I guess Although maybe that's it...not focusing on any one in particular. Like dual dishnet setups.

    I wonder though if my head will pop and I'll go crazy if I fill it too full with too much of this shit...like that Chinese guy somewhere that said that thing about feeling connected to everyone but feeling lonely on a mountain top or something....becoming a stranger to himself/

    Ok, shut up brain, you're done for the day. All the homeworks done, a book buried deep into, college ap completings going on...I need cartoons...or even something VanWilderish could do. And some of that annie orgo peace pasta n cheese, which I must admit is yummier than first thought. Be open to new things Simon. Oooo, and selflove to the thought of someone special...hmm nameless and faceless but amorous anyways, the person I can't identify but who I know will come by in time when least expect it. ... ok. Not expecting it now. Not in the least. Hello??? ... Hey! Where are you?!? ☺

    Hmm...or I could just go with the super pretty picture that comes from the thought of field hockey one-N-ed Jen. Yea, it's time.

Hmm...why can't she be both?   ;)

One N hockey Jen

Antiblog de simon

9-13-04 3:50pm

Whoa, found this on some dudes LJ blog:::::

  "the only people for me are the mad ones, the ones who are mad to live, mad to talk, mad to be saved, desirous of everything at the same time, the only ones who never yawn or say a common place thing, but burn burn like the fabulous yellow roman candles exploding live spiders across the stars and in the middle you see the blue centerlight pop and everybody goes, 'awww!'" - Jack Kerouac

The super sum-it-up quote from a crazy fucking maniac man from Mass who found himself on the road half century ago but with my angsty focus and attention span, contempt of collective corruption, appreciation of awe, and trying to navigate in between. You go Jack! Throw a few back. Cheers!

     Hopefully though I could content myself with substances that don't have to go to the extreme of that poor bloke. I get pissy when I feel trapped into this bullshit often nightmarish idea of what's real, but a little coffee or wine and people like this wacked out Kero-Wack are enough to make me think and wonder if there's hope, since its so fucking apparent that it is bullshit now...time to wake up?? Well fuck the nightmares makers that are the fools around here, I'm going to get some cool dreamings on and make em real. CEST LA VIE BABY!

     So I think I'm going to ask Mr. Alverez for advice on how to do that independent study option that us double-dippers are into. Maybe something some cool cross cultural history stuff like what Ashad was talking about getting on. So far, this shit in class is way too easy and Ashad working on his proposal really has my mind peaked for it and not settling for mediocre. Well, not mediocre, but smaller steps already stepped. Even if I failed them.. Makes me wish I wouldn't have flunked this back in the beginning. But fuck I learn more with chats with people like him and Tracey that I do in class lectures. How fucked up is that? But at least with all the slow shifted downtime at work and the slowly working through the Karamazovs, I'll get into the groove about the 20th Cent of BS. The title now. Yes. I'm going to do it. Deep pool parts for Simon! Especially bout the especially post WWII and post CW being too fucking similar in the, oh shit, lets find someone to scare people with. Would be kick ass to bust out with the worldly tie-in shit like Russian history and how it ties into the American shit and the prop they were both throwing around and actually also the Israeli bullshit prop here and now as well...with all the shit going on. Seriously! That's what I'm doing... And then boom I can hand the shit out to everyone in that class at the end of the year and drop the bullshit bomb on them. Nice little present to the youngans. BooYow. Yo. Nooo....Yow.

    Dude...seriously...Only three classes needed for the big ol gradumawaytion...so cool.

    I'm just so fucking intrigued that this peasant/aristo Russian shit FD goes into feels so similarto the here and now shit. Russian peasant...and what? American urban hick? Well, that's not fair, just like judging BSGW on a personal level based on his misfiredpolicy when not having ever met the bloke but as much as on a job level he's going to get his ass fired I'll stop calling him a fucking moron on a personal level. Maybe just a sad soul that never grown out and up...but when a half-your-age gay IranianBritboy can get past all the shit thrown at him and become a better person and know better than you, good thing its time to clock out of the office and clock into yourself.

    Damnnnn...way lost, where the hell was i...so withholding judgment on that level, well same way I guess I can't go urban hick across the board, but the dude sure as hell reminds me of all the prettyboy military types shooting up all the freaky everything in MIB. How bout, a B+ for effort, but wide of the target, sorry, in the end C- at best, you can't proceed to the next level. Me with French. Moi avec frances. Avec or chez? Or au or aux? Ah fuck it. But yea... Monsieur Bush avec responsabilite et autorite sur les autres, or something like that... so its like the fucked up GOP 'takeover' Ashad was saying, a few thousand people difference allows the Grand Old PoliceStaters a decade of monkey wrenching. So nearly every year of my life on this third rock has been veiled in bullshit.

    Thanks for the veil dance Liz and Tom.

    So what is it, 21st century American middle/peasant class overall and then the urban hick being the gun freaky, rightwingy bastards that are glee happy with their peasantness and willing to help the big bush boys keep them that way so they can feel all big and bad but go passive and expect it to be given to them a-la American History X? . There you are American urban neopeasant hicks, how is being happy with tiny ass tax break for yourself and then accepting school budget cuts different than the poor serf bastards being happy getting paid in vodka and then not getting anything or help and not even a ruble or kopek when their roof starts leaking or kid gets sick. Just a matter of figuring our shit out here and there and keep us all from falling down the slippery muddy slope to the pig shit slop where all the urban hicks somehow like to hang out. And how to convince the rest of the world there is a difference and to throw us a rope. aLittle Help!?? Cheers, thanks.......

    So fuck ya! I'm all down with the rest of the neopeasant Americans!! 100million strong, who want to do shit that could make their lives better, not down with the same piano loop, over and over, so done with it, but still without the time, but it'll all get smooth, we'll all be cool. We can all work it, We can all sing... All races many faces, any religions all faiths true United States of America emerging big, feel small, giving props to the sixbillion strong super United States of all us Wicked Bass-tads of this big ball, and mad props my music mixing me going all crystalballers followed by dude dissing backstreet brawlers, So, mad props to the masters, TEB and the Streets, putting these beats into my head as I type some shit and go all unconventional and multidimensional....disillusioned overworked but underpayed outsourced super-debted but all so promising and potentialed...oh here comes the changeover, busting out with the transcendence via the bring me to life evanescence...

Go Neopeasant and come into your own. Name it your own, not against any other... realize its for all, psycho to soulful, street smarts or book smarts, but can't have it skated by or any other way... bit of assignment here, practice and exercise, glorious results, commonsense and coolness for bird and blokes, its for all of us, so lets push things forward..

I'm at home about to go to work while the ball boys practice outside on a pretty day. And I'm smiling and satisfied. They got theirs. I got mine. Time to Push things forward. I'm superchilled and feeling my way through the stress and through the schooling until I emerge outside and into a great new divide.

Once bitten, forever smitten.

Forever smitten

P.S.

Keeping it simple and Simon-style - he said it best himself referencing or quoting the words or works of others:

...once bitten, forever smitten.

: Rock on es!!
: Thanks for the props Alvy and G...don't know what to say, but suppose...
: With that layup I'll just say to ya'll...
:
: BITE ME!!!!!
: LOL!
: Now go bite each other!
: But yea...
: So obvious love yous and miss yous allaround but gotta go with the overall...
: But I'm so with the cool Alvy on his shit at the start. Damn straight!!
: To hell with all of you who'll doll me up and exile me to a corner of your unlived-in living room in a five dollar frame...pushpin me to some corner of your corkboard for a dorm-room year or two while you get your shit schooled and but try to look like you're a badass and got it all together.
: WTF...probably exiling me next to some lameass cutout cliche about people leaving footprints in your heart or some shit so you don't feel out of touch or unsure about yourself since you haven't talked to yours in so long??? FUCK YOU! SLC Punk-style! Boom...one last ref!
: Who would have bet on that being the one? :)
: Seriously though...

: Live your life.
: Live it well.
: Learn to listen to each other, so you can become each other.
: Which you already are.
:

: Trust me on that one. O:-)
: You see all the wicked and crazy cool peeps I know...that I am now. 8-)
:
: That's all you gotta do.
: All Ya'll are God's gift. But you know there's a sense of humor, up There and Everywhere...
: So you gotta go be the Tool you know you are,
:
: It isn't that hard.
: Just try to be down with yourself...
: And don't stop.
: Capitalize yourself. capital T BabY!!
:
:
: Its just this:
:
: We're all teammates.
: Play your hearts out
: Live it up!
: Live it well!
: And leave it all on the field!
: Only then are you your own MVP, only then are we all MVPs.
:
: HA I'm the peptalker now!!
:
:
: OMG!! G2G
: Got some crazy new shit to take care of and get into!!!

: Peace ;)